D0519322

The Marigolds Make Good

BLACKIE & SON LIMITED
16/18 William IV Street, Charing Cross, LONDON, W.C.2
17 Stanhope Street, GLASGOW

BLACKIE & SON (INDIA) LIMITED
103/5 Fort Street, BOMBAY

BLACKIE & SON (CANADA) LIMITED
TORONTO

R.H.BROCK

F21

MEETING LADY ROYSTON!
Page 43

Frontispiece

The
Marigolds Make Good

BY

CATHERINE CHRISTIAN

Author of "Cherries in Search of a Captain"

With frontispiece

BLACKIE & SON LIMITED
LONDON AND GLASGOW

To

L. J. Hetley

Who has been to an older Patrol
what Lady Royston proved to the Marigolds

Printed in Great Britain by Blackie & Son, Ltd., Glasgow

THE MARIGOLDS MAKE GOOD

CHAPTER I

A Bolt from the Blue

" Suspend the School Guide Company? Suspend it until the autumn anyway and perhaps for always? Oh, Miss Nesbitt, you *can't* do a thing like that!"

The most junior patrol leader in St. Bridget's Guides stared, white faced, across the table in the prefects' common room at the new head-mistress. A little rustle went round the table, as the school prefects, and the other two patrol leaders, turned to look at the speaker. Miss Blagrove, the Guide captain, seated at the head-mistress's right hand, took off her horn-rimmed glasses, and said mildly:

" Don't interrupt, Norah—you haven't heard all Miss Nesbitt has to say."

Norah subsided, pushing back her heavy, red-gold plaits restlessly. She was a thin, athletic fifteen-year-old, with a pale face, grey eyes, and a wide, sensitive mouth that could be both impudent and appealing.

Miss Nesbitt looked at her understandingly.

" I'm sorry—very sorry—to suggest closing down," she said. " But, you see, all of us have got to put the school and the good of the school before our private likes and dislikes for the next six months, girls, if we mean to keep St. Bridget's going, and uphold its fine tradition. You do understand that, don't you?"

Five prefects and three patrol leaders nodded solemnly. There was something so terribly logical and sensible about the tall, dark-haired, dark-eyed young head-mistress, that St. Bridget's seniors, who, for two years had sadly lacked a firm hand on the reins of school government, looked to her with a confidence they themselves hardly realized.

" If I weren't an old St. Bridget's girl myself, I might not mind quite so much about pulling things together," Miss Nesbitt went on. " When I was at school here, fifteen years ago (Miss Blagrove remembers it as well as I do—she'll tell you the same thing), St. Bridget's examination results were only outshone by St. Bridget's successes on the playing field." Miss Nesbitt paused. Her prefects shifted a little uneasily in their seats. The three patrol leaders looked at one another. They were all remembering the same things. The things that had not, really, been anybody's fault, but had happened because Miss Wilmott, founder and for fifty years head-mistress of the school, had been failing in health, and the school buildings were old-fashioned and cramped—much too small for the numbers of new girls pouring in each term from the outskirts of the town, where a whole colony of houses had recently been built around the big aerodrome.

Somehow or other, St. Bridget's had lost its grip. Seventeen failures out of twenty had marked the last matriculation as a massacre; and the hockey and lacrosse teams were making the loss of every match a foregone conclusion. Miss Wilmott, in the Christmas term, had given up the struggle, and taken to her bed. In January Miss Nesbitt had arrived, unostentatious, but efficient, and since then St. Bridget's had wondered rather dizzily just what was going to happen next.

Actually it was red-haired Irish Norah who had nicknamed her " The Thunderbolt "—for Miss Nesbitt's reforms fell out of a clear sky—when she moved in school affairs it was always quickly, unexpectedly, and often, as in this present case of the school Guide Company, with devastating results. So far, though some of them had electrified her pupils, the reforms she had instituted had met with their entire approval. This time, however, Norah, if no one else, was moved to protest. She murmured rebelliously, under her breath:

" In those days St. Bridget's Guide Company was marvellous too—it won the County Banner in 1920—I know it did."

Miss Nesbitt and Miss Blagrove exchanged glances. Miss Nesbitt's smile was inscrutable. Miss Blagrove flushed a little and looked appealingly at the Head.

" Perhaps we could manage one meeting every week—or even a fortnight?" she suggested.

Miss Nesbitt shook her head.

" It isn't fair on you, Miss Blagrove. You've got far too much to do this term, as it is, with tennis coaching and swimming classes and so on each evening. The Guides can't expect to take up your valuable time any more—at any rate, for a month or so. We decided that before."

" Some of them are quite keen," Miss Blagrove murmured, apologetically.

" Well—perhaps they are." Miss Nesbitt agreed. " But just a few members of the Camera Club and the Nature Society and the Geological Group, and the Sketching Club—just a few—appear to have been keen, too. I've been ruthless with them. I've washed out *all* the school societies completely, as you know — and you prefects voted that I should, didn't you?"

They nodded. Vivian Bond, the head girl, said soberly:

" We'd got too many societies. We were cluttered up with them. They hadn't justified their existence for terms and terms."

" Exactly." Miss Nesbitt turned her sudden keen glance full on Norah and the other two leaders. Perhaps by accident her hand went to the lapel of her tailored coat, and she turned it so that the shining silver trefoil pinned on the inner side showed for a moment: " Do you feel, any one of you three, that St. Bridget's Guides have justified their existence lately—justified all the time and trouble Miss Blagrove

has to spend on the company, and the main gym-
room being given over to them twice a week, and the
big cupboard for their equipment in the locker room
—can you show me any reason why the school will
be poorer without a company, in fact?"

Madge Davis, the senior leader, rubbed her fair
fringe up on end, and said rather plaintively:

" Really, Miss Nesbitt, I can't see we've done
anything——"

" You haven't!" Miss Nesbitt caught her up quickly,
the sentence unfinished. " That's just what I complain
about, Madge. Out of three hundred girls in this
school, less than twenty belong to the Guide Company
—and out of those twenty, often seven or eight fail
to turn up at the meeting because it clashes with one
or other of the multifarious activities of school societies.
That's no exaggeration, is it?"

" I'm afraid it isn't, Miss Nesbitt," Madge admitted.
" We have been rather slack—at least," she added,
frowning in a puzzled way, " I think we've been more
muddled, really—there never seems time for everything."

" That's exactly what I feel," Miss Nesbitt agreed
seriously. " Now, I want you all to have a chance to
start afresh and decide what you really *do* want to do
with your spare time, after you have given all the
mind you possess to your school work and sports in
turn. I hate dither, and I hate inefficiency. Both
these things are just bad habits—but like all bad
habits, they're much harder to get out of than into.

There's going to be only one watchword for us all, if we mean to pull St. Bridget's out of the rut, my dears—*concentration*. I know it's very hard, and I don't like doing it (for I was enrolled, and worked right through the ranks in St. Bridget's myself, remember) but I am going to close down the company this week—and whether it ever opens again will depend on circumstances and yourselves. Perhaps when the new buildings are finished in September, if you can show me any really good reason for doing it, I might re-consider the situation. Has anyone anything to say?"

No one seemed to have. Norah, staring very hard at a fly which was wading through a jungle of long hairs in the green baize table cloth, wondered miserably *why* she had never made the Marigold Patrol work harder. Perhaps if some of them were First Class, or had their all-round cords—perhaps if they had thought to help more with school functions, instead of mad-rabbiting off to the woods on every fine Saturday afternoon—perhaps? She winked angrily, as the fly suddenly wavered into a mist of sharp, pricking tears. She stood up with the rest, while Miss Nesbitt left them, Miss Blagrove following her from the room.

Madge, her fringe like a cockatoo-tuft, turned to Alice, the Cornflower leader, a dark, sallow girl of fourteen:

" Well, that's the end of us for a bit—and a good thing too, in some ways. I'll be thankful to get rid of the fag of a patrol for the next little while, until my exam's over in July," she confessed.

Alice nodded:

" It'll be quite fun, having Friday evenings free for a bit—and I bet the company *will* start again in the autumn term."

" Why should it?" Norah asked abruptly. She felt suddenly overwhelmingly unhappy, and she wanted to vent it on the others, who were taking things so casually—so cavalierly. " Why should the company start again, ever and ever, unless we do something about it? Do you imagine if we'd been a proper sort of a company Miss Nesbitt would have closed us down? She's a Guide herself, and she understands about things."

" Here, steady on." Vivian, the head girl, attracted by Norah's violence, joined the group. " You aren't being closed down as an awful disgrace or punishment, Norah—you do exaggerate so. Miss Nesbitt hasn't time, or room, for a Guide Company until the school's got through the next six months. That's all."

" It isn't all. You know it isn't," Norah said impetuously. " We may not be being closed down for a punishment, but it's our own faults the school can do without a company. We ought to have made Guides just indispensable. We've never really *worked*— never."

" Save us, listen to the child!" Patricia Ellis, a pretty, blue - eyed prefect cut in teasingly. " This sort of earnestness is admirable. I thought Guiding was a recreation, not a vocation?"

"Well, that's where you're jolly well wrong." Norah's grey-green eyes blazed suddenly. "Real Guiding isn't only a recreation. The Knights of Arthur weren't knights for fun, were they? It's because we've all been thinking of Guiding as an alternative to bug-hunting, or fossil-grubbing, or—or messing around with developing negatives, that we've lost our company—and I think it's perfectly awful—that's all."

"If you feel as bad as all that about it, you'd better reform the rest of the company," Prudence Norton, the spectacled and sarcastic president of the now-dissolved Geological Society suggested. "You might start on manners—I seem to have heard a Guide is supposed to be courteous—'bug-hunting' and 'fossil-grubbing' doesn't strike me as the politest way to refer to other people's hobbies."

Norah bit her lip and Vivian, who was really a conscientious head girl and hated quarrels, interrupted more kindly than tactfully:

"Seriously, you patrol leaders, if you want Miss Nesbitt to re-open the company you'd better get your patrols in hand and make good before September. Can't you work up for some of your badges, or do some special good deeds or something?"

Madge shook her head:

"I don't think my patrol will want to do much. Most of them are exam-ing for dear life this term."

"So are mine—and Lilian and Marie are in the

team—They'll be glad to be free of active Guiding," Alice agreed.

Vivian, a little crestfallen, looked at Norah. Norah was gazing through the window at the grey clouds, hurrying across the March sky. She seemed rather wistful and aloof, but a spark had kindled a long way back in her grey eyes. Answering Vivian's unspoken question with a disarming vagueness she said slowly:

" My patrol's not much good at exams—or at games. Matter of fact, we aren't 'specially brainy lot at anything, Vivian, when I come to think about it. But I'll talk to them about what you suggest—one never knows—they might quite like to ' make good ' if they thought about it."

CHAPTER II

The Jolly Roger

"This," said Norah impressively, some hours later, "is where the Marigold Patrol begins to *be* a patrol."

The remark might have been more impressive if the wheel-barrow, on whose handle she had perched herself, had not chosen that moment to tip up, sliding her gently on to the floor of the tool shed, with her long legs straight out in front of her, and her long plaits straight up behind.

Patsy, Bridget and Pixie greeted the interruption with relief. Not because they objected to their patrol leader's habit of making startling and dramatic statements, but because the evening had been so far such an exceedingly unpleasant one that they were inclined to welcome any event which lightened the gloom.

"If you ask me, it's where the Marigold Patrol gets off the bus—once for all, completely, absolutely and entirely," Patsy Ormonde groaned, while the two younger ones helped Norah up again and brushed her down solicitously.

"Sure it's where we get off the bus." Norah twisted herself almost double in order to investigate the damage to her short Guide uniform skirt. "Isn't that just exactly what I was demonstrating to the lot of you? And who wants to stay on a bus, anyway? Isn't a bus just the dullest, deadliest thing you ever saw, chugging itself along the main roads, stopping and starting, stopping and starting every five minutes. Tell me just this, now—when we've been out hiking, the four of us, hasn't the fun begun, and only just begun, where we got off the bus?"

She gazed round at the other three challengingly.

Patsy, older by six months and shorter by a head than her P.L., pushed her hand upwards through her already ruffled short crop until the wavy auburn hair stood out like a burning bush.

"I don't see what you're getting at, Norah," she complained. "You've been slanging us up hill and down dale ever since we got here, for being so slack that the company was counted in as one of the silly little odd things the school can do without during alterations—and then you say we're just going to begin some enormously exciting adventure. What do you mean about it all?"

Norah flopped into the wheel barrow and hung her legs comfortably over its high green side. She had begun to whistle soundlessly, and her eyes held a far-away look.

The two younger members of her patrol watched her anxiously. The Marigold Patrol only numbered four, beside Norah and Patsy there was Biddie, Patsy's thirteen-year-old sister—a square-built, freckled, dependable person, with straight, sandy hair, cut in a

fringed bob, and Pixie who, at twelve, was still something of a spoilt baby, with curly hair the deep shiny
copper of an old warming-pan, and very big blue eyes,
with long lashes.

Miss Blagrove had christened them " The Marigold
Patrol " the first time she saw their red heads all in a
line. They had accepted the title joyfully, and been on
the look out, ever since, for red-haired recruits. But
none had appeared, until Mary Glover, small and shy
and short-sighted, came as a new girl into Biddie
Ormonde's form at St. Bridget's and unexpectedly
announced that she would like to join the Guides.

It was remarkably hard luck on Mary that the very
week she should have been enrolled was the week the
company was closing down, Biddie reflected, as she
waited for Norah to go on speaking.

After what seemed a long pause, Norah said slowly:
" My idea is this. We've been playing at Guides
this last two years—not being Guides. I didn't see
it, until Miss Nesbitt talked to us. But I do see it now.
Captain's a perfect dear, and the most understanding
person I've ever met, but just because she's so understanding, she's spoilt us. She's always let us off things,
and taken our excuses, and tried to make all the work part
of Guiding easy for us. Why, we've never even camped
except at the standing camp site at Burnt Ashe, where
all the difficult bits are done for you before you start.
I hardly know how to pitch a tent, and I certainly
couldn't find my way by the stars, and if anybody
had a bad accident when I was alone with them they'd

probably die, because I hardly remember a bit about first aid. We're just tenderfoots through and through and through, and the sooner we admit it, the better."

"Well, suppose we are, what do we *do* about it?" Patsy asked, rather ruffled.

"Get back to beginnings and start afresh," Norah answered briskly. "The first Guides didn't have elaborate camps and lectures on the tests, and loads of books to study from *and* Guiders to nurse and mother and maiden-aunt them. They just jolly well started out with a copy of *Scouting for Boys* and their own common sense, and learned how to *do* things."

"Oh, Norah, couldn't we do that?" Pixie asked eagerly, the romance of the idea appealing to her.

"It's what we are going to do," Norah told her grimly. "Vivian talked about 'making good'. Well, I've more than an idea we're going to 'make bad' —very bad—from her point of view, because we aren't going to be proper and conventional and uplifted at all. If we start out on our own, what we do will have about as much resemblance to Vivian's idea of Guiding, as Drake's expedition to Panama had to naval discipline of his day."

"What expedition was that?" Patsy asked, puzzled.

"Oh, a lovely story!" Norah hugged her knees. "Drake went off and sacked Panama, and nobody else but he himself and Queen Elizabeth knew he was under orders from her. All the admirals of the fleet thought he'd deserted and turned into a pirate—I'll tell you about it properly some time. If we start to do really-truly wood-crafty, adventurous, Red Indiany sort of things everybody will think *we've* turned pirates too—you see if they don't. All except Captain and Miss Nesbitt, that is. Miss Nesbitt's like Queen Elizabeth, I think—the Queen never gave people orders, exactly, she gave them opportunities, instead. If they took them, she was pleased, and if they never saw there was one there at all to take, she was just immensely bored, and never took any notice of that person again."

" Like Madge and Alice," Pixie put in with self-righteous enjoyment. " They aren't going to do anything, you said so, Norah——"

" Maybe they aren't, and maybe they are—that's not our business," Norah rebuked her, with a grin. " What we've got to do is plan how best we can start to work ourselves. We're jolly lucky to have this place to meet in, to begin with—your Daddie is a sport to let us come here, Pat."

Pat looked pleased.

" I dare say he'd help us in other ways if we asked him," she said eagerly. " He's often said he'd teach us first aid and home nursing if we wanted to learn— only he couldn't do it at regular times, because, being a doctor, he gets called out so much."

" I know—but it's an idea, all the same, and awfully kind of him."

Norah got out of the wheelbarrow with one deft twist of her whole body and going over to the door, looked out at the strip of garden, where the tall spring grass needed cutting, and the sticky buds of the poplar trees smelt clean and exciting after the rain.

" If only we knew the first thing about gardening we might try to prove we really are grateful to him for everything by making things grow in this garden," she added.

" Daddie would just love that," Biddie put in. " He adores tidy gardens—but he never has time to do much himself and neither has Mummie, and Patsy and I get bored with it—and we can't afford a gardener, at any rate not while Tony's at college. Do you really think we could garden sometimes, Norah?"

" We could try!" Norah turned, and her face was suddenly very grave. " There just isn't anything we can't have a good shot at, if we stick together and really work. Listen to me, all of you—it's such waste to play about and pretend to be Guides, when we can perfectly well start from to-day to *be* Guides. I don't want to make good for what we can get out of it—as a sort of bribe to Miss Nesbitt to let us have a company again. I want to do it as an experiment, for the fun and the adventure. Let's hoist the Jolly Roger— ' death but no surrender '—and sail into unknown seas, and bring back such a cargo that we'll be knighted instead of hanged, same as Drake was. Oh, don't you see what fun it's going to be?"

They saw. It was impossible not to see when Norah got carried away with an enthusiasm.

Coming down to earth with one of her startling changes of mood, she glanced at her watch.

" Glory—it's awfully late! I must fly—and so must you, young Pixie, or your Mother'll think you've been kidnapped. Listen, people, to-morrow's Saturday. I vote we put on our oldest clothes and take our tea with us, and go off on an ' explore '. There's a bus to Hadley Wood starting from the station at two o'clock. We may as well begin as we mean to go on, and adventures don't just happen—they didn't even happen to Lancelot and Tristram and that lot—unless ' they ridden forth to meet with them '—the book says so. Can you all come to-morrow?"

" Rather!" three voices answered simultaneously.

" Good!" Norah picked up her haversack and hat, glanced round her patrol and added solemnly:

" The Jolly Roger's our flag, remember. ' Death but no surrender '. From now on we're a pirate crew. Pixie, if you don't hurry, I'll order you to walk the plank!"

CHAPTER III

Mary Glover, Volunteer

" Somebody to see me, Mother? Who is it?"

Norah, curled up in the sunny window-seat of her room the following morning, with Hakluyt's *Voyages* spread out on her knee, and *The Book of Woodcraft* on the floor beside her, looked up without enthusiasm at the prospect of an interruption.

Mrs. Morrison, a pretty, fragile little woman, with prematurely greying hair, shook her head:

" I don't know, dear—quite a child—I've never seen her before. I think she said her name was Glover."

" What—Mary Glover? I wonder whatever she wants?"

In one spring Norah was off the window-seat and half way across the floor:

" Bring her up to your room, dear, will you, if you want to talk?" Mrs. Morrison begged. " Your father is in the library, and Milly is turning out the dining-room. I'll send you up two cups of cocoa in a minute —the child looks starvy to me!"

" Mummie, you're a darling!" Norah caught and hugged her Mother in passing. " I believe if the

king called you'd want to sit him down ' to-a-real-
proper-meal-poor-man ', now, wouldn't you?"

"Don't talk nonsense," Mrs. Morrison said briskly,
but her eyes twinkled. There was, she admitted,
quite a grain of truth in the accusation.

Norah was down the stairs in three bounds, and
smiling her most friendly Irish smile at the rather
derelict-looking little figure in the hall.

Mary Glover was eleven, and small for her age.
Her hair—passport to the Marigold Patrol—hung in
whisps round her pale face, and was the variety of
red called, inevitably, " carrots ". It was, apparently,
in process of growing, and had reached the awkward
stage when, too long to look tidy, it still refused to
keep in place with the tightest of stringy hair-ribbons,
despairingly tugged in at the back of the neck. Steel-
rimmed spectacles, perched rather crookedly on an
inconspicuous nose gave their wearer a definitely
comic appearance, from which the fact that her new
coat and hat of St. Bridget's green were several sizes
too large for her did not detract. In spite of this
unpromising exterior there was something staunch
and plucky about the child that had attracted Norah
to her from the first, and there was genuine warmth
in her voice as she said:

"Come up to my room, Mary."

Silently Mary followed her upstairs and stood just
inside the door, looking round the gay, sun-drenched
place, with its pretty chintzes, modern furniture,
painted pale powder blue, with little bunches of

flowers on it, and the big bowl of pink hyacinths on
the low bookcase.

" Oh, what a lovely room!" she said breathlessly.

" It is nice, isn't it?" Norah agreed, pleased with the
compliment. " Mummie re-furnished it for my last
birthday, and I do love the new furniture," she added,
laughing a little shyly, " I suppose really I'm awfully
lucky."

" Yes," Mary said simply, with a sigh of intense
admiration. Then she suddenly seemed to pull herself
together, and said abruptly: " Please, is it true that
there isn't going to be a Guide Company at school
any more?"

Norah made a face.

" Sorry, old thing, I'm afraid it is," she admitted.
" Miss Nesbitt means to announce the fact officially
on Monday morning. I didn't think you'd hear until
then."

" Captain told me. I went round to her house last
night, to tell her Mother couldn't afford my uniform
yet, and she told me that the head-mistress was s'pend-
ing Guides until further notice. But I don't see how
you can s'pend Guides, really, do you?"

Norah looked at the solemn little face curiously.

" How do you mean, Mary? We aren't to have any
more meetings until September—perhaps not then."

" Yes, but meetings aren't Guides," Mary persisted
cheerfully. " Not any more than uniform is. Uniform's
nice, and so are meetings, but they aren't the 'sential
parts of Guiding, are they?"

Decidedly taken aback, Norah stared at her recruit.

" Now who taught you that, I wonder?" she meditated. " It's what I've been saying, loud and long, for about three years, but I doubt if even Patsy has taken it in, so far. Where did you get the hang of things from, young Mary?"

" Chief Scout," said Mary promptly. " I've read every single one of his books. I'd read a lot before I came here, and I found the rest in the Junior Public Library. Then, of course, I had Mother's *How Girls Can Help to Build the Empire*. I read that when I was seven, and I've played at bits out of it ever since."

" Was your mother a Guide, then?" Norah asked. Mary nodded.

" Yes," she added conscientiously. " She is still, of course. She says you can't stop being, once you've been enrolled. You can only be a bad Guide, or a good Guide—because you do promise for always, don't you?"

" You do," Norah agreed.

She moved across to a tray that the maid had just brought in:

" Suppose you drink this cocoa, and eat some biscuits before you talk any more philosophy! By the way, what did Captain say to all your theories?"

" Not an awful lot," Mary admitted. She curled her fingers round the warmth of the cup, absentmindedly. Norah saw that, though inky, they were thin and sensitive. " She said, if I liked, she'd recommend me to one of the other companies in Oakleigh, because there wasn't any reason why St. Bridget's girls shouldn't belong to companies outside the school."

" Well?" Norah questioned.

" I asked her if the Marigolds were going to another company, and when she said, not as far as she knew, I said then of course I couldn't, because a person can't be enrolled without a person's patrol, can one?" and Mary beamed, suddenly and disarmingly, as though the explanation ended all argument.

Norah sat down limply.

" Either you're most frightfully brainy, or else you're quite daft, and I suppose as you won a scholarship it must be that you're clever," she said weakly. " But you positively addle my brain! If you went to a new company you wouldn't be in our patrol—I mean we shouldn't be your patrol—I mean—oh, don't you *see*, Mary?"

Mary shook her head. Her face was devoid of all expression as a small owl's.

" I belong in your patrol, and unless you're going anywhere different, I'm not," she announced obstinately, and added, brightening, " look at my hair!"

" Hmph—well, that certainly does stamp you as a Marigold in one sense," Norah chuckled, the humour of the situation beginning to dawn on her.

Mary buried her nose in her cup, came out of it with a frank sigh of satisfaction, and asked, as one sure of her answer:

" You are going to go on being a patrol, aren't you?"

" Well, as a matter of fact, we are," Norah admitted.

" Captain said she thought you would."

" Oh, *did* she?" Norah inquired, a little taken aback. " Now I wonder what the dickens made her so certain about that? The others aren't—the Cornflowers and Heathers, I mean."

" No—that's because they're bigger than we are, and have exams and things, Captain said. But she said she betted her Sunday hat the Marigolds wouldn't let her down."

" Let her down?" Norah queried thoughtfully. " Let *her* down, you say?"

Mary Glover flushed, and nodded.

" That's what she said—but maybe I ought not to have repeated it. I thought maybe you'd fixed things up with her, though—I didn't understand——"

" That's all right, Mary," suddenly Norah laughed. " You've let the cat out of the bag all right, my child, but it's the sort of cat I'm glad to be sure about at this moment—I somehow thought Captain wasn't so keen to get rid of us all—Oh, well—But what a lark that we'd made up our minds to carry on, anyway! Queen Elizabeth must have been relieved when she heard Drake had sailed without orders."

" What do you mean exactly, please, Norah?" Mary was puzzled.

" Never you mind—not for the moment, anyway. Look here, if you really want to be a Marigold, you can be, but you won't be enrolled for ages and ages, and you won't be able to wear uniform, and you'll

have to work jolly hard, because we've all decided to
the next bit of time. It won't be like belonging to an
ordinary company at all—but I think it may be fun.
Do you want to try?"

"Yes, please," Mary said simply. Suddenly her
eyes twinkled behind her glasses, and she quoted
sedately, " ' I am willing, sir, though I be in fact a
Gentleman Adventurer, to haul and draw along with
the common Sailor Men '."

"Oh, you are, are you?" Taken aback for the
second time, Norah chuckled at this apt and unexpected
capping of her own allusion to Drake. "That isn't
at all how it comes in the book, my child—but it
means the same thing. You read a lot, do you?"

"Lots," Mary agreed. " I've adored reading about
adventures, specially, ever since I was little. But,"
she added fervently, " I'd much rather really be in
one, than read about them."

"Well, I dare say you will be in a good few if you
join up with us," Norah predicted, and added, reflectively: "At any rate, it won't be my fault if you
aren't, I can tell you that."

CHAPTER IV

A Wrong to be Righted

" Mary is definitely brainy, and she's having rather a thin time, from what I can gather," Norah confided to Patsy, as the two of them swung along the lane to Hadley Woods that afternoon, their longer legs carrying them well ahead of the rest of the patrol.

" You know she came to St. Bridget's on a scholarship, don't you?" Patsy asked.

" Yes. Apparently her father died last year and her mother's got a job in London, but they were both awfully keen she should have a good education, so she worked like anything for the open schol: she's boarding with some people in Neville Road."

" I know—Biddie went to call for her before Guides, the first meeting she came to, and said it was ever such a depressing house—very gloomy, with torn lace curtains, and the front steps all broken away. There aren't any other young people living there."

Norah nodded.

" That's what I gathered, though she didn't grumble at all. You see, Pat, I wondered at first if it was quite fair to let her enlist with outlaws like us, when I suppose she could still get into a good, solid company. We

can't enrol her or anything, and the poor kid won't
even be allowed to wear her uniform, if she ever gets
it, but afterwards I thought maybe she'd have more
fun with us. We shall *do* more—and we can teach
her things, so that the minute the company starts
again she can be enrolled and she'll get her second
class at once then."

In spite of herself Pat sighed.

" Seems a long time to September, doesn't it?"
she asked, with rather a wry smile.

" Not when you think of all we mean to do in
between." Norah, her hands deep in the pockets of
her old green blazer, shuffled the white March dust
and glanced up at the beech trees in the hedge, their
delicate, sheath-like buds bursting in the afternoon
sun. " I'd like to qualify for horse-woman and rifle-
shot and pioneer, and pathfinder, and all the badges
nobody ever thinks of getting, wouldn't you? I'm
sick of doing things I know how to do——"

Patsy grimaced.

" I'm much more sick of failing needlewoman's—I've
failed it three times," she admitted. " It's hanging me
up for first class."

" But more than getting any badges I'd like to learn
Indian lore, and sort of gipsy things." Norah turned,
waved to the three small figures toiling a hundred
yards behind, and uttered an unexpected shout of
encouragement to them. " *Oi-ee*, you-all—hurry!
I've got an idea!"

" What about?" Patsy asked, decidedly startled.

" A scrumptious idea!" Norah stretched out her arms, as though wanting to fly. In her green clothes, with the wind blowing her skirt and her long plaits, she looked as if she might easily turn into a bird. Patsy, in her neat brown jersey and skirt, with a brown beret pulled over her tidy, cropped head would certainly have been taken for the more responsible of the two at that moment.

But Biddie and Pixie, who knew their leader, broke into a run, anxious not to miss any fun that might be going, and Mary panted breathlessly behind them, her black kilt and rather grubby white polo jersey making her look younger and skinnier than ever.

" Listen!" Norah began the moment they were within ear shot. " Do you remember old Gipsy Ellie who sold the bunches of waterlilies to us that day last summer, when we came here with Captain?"

" Yes!"

Three heads nodded, and Mary stared interestedly through her crooked glasses.

" Well, you know Captain told us then that she was an honest-to-goodness real gipsy, not just a tramp? She lives in a hut somewhere in Hadley Wood, and if we could find it I know she could teach us loads and loads of things. Gipsies know all about animals and plants and herbs, and they know how to make baskets and lay marvellous trails. Maybe she'd teach us how to recognize gipsy trails—' paterans ' as they call them. Shall we go and ask her?"

" Oh, Norah, *dare* you?" Pixie looked rather scared.

(F 21)

" 'Course! I expect she'll be pleased to see somebody to talk to—and maybe we could bring her some tobacco and sweets next time—I wish I'd thought of that to-day. But I've got a quarter of a pound of tea I bought, because on the way to the bus I found I'd left mine behind—that'll do to break the ice with."

" And you can have half mine at tea time," Biddie put in—and added eagerly, " I'd willingly go without any to get old Gipsy Ellie to talk to us. I want to learn about herbs more than anything—Daddie talked about them to me. D'you know where her hut is?"

" Well, not exactly," Norah admitted. " But I've a pretty good idea. We go in by the gate at the top of this hill, you know, where we went with Captain, and then there's a path that leads down into the wood. Ellie's hut is somewhere by the stream, I believe."

" But——" Pat hesitated. " You know, Norah, that bit of the wood's private. Captain got permission to take us there because she knew Lady Royston. Do you think we ought——?"

" Sure, what harm is it going to do Lady Royston if we walk through her wood, then?" Norah purposely broadened her attractive Irish accent. " Any way, she won't know, because she hasn't lived at Stone House for years. It was the housekeeper Captain used to ring up for permission—I'd have done the same if I'd thought of it, but I didn't, and I'm not going back now, or we shall waste all the afternoon. If we meet a keeper I'll explain—but I don't suppose we shall, because with Lady Royston always living in

London I expect they're pretty slack. We never saw one with Captain, did we?"

Pat had to admit they never did. Norah laughed at the somewhat grudging and worried fashion in which she nodded assent.

" I told you yesterday we were going to ' make bad '. Trespassing's a very good way to begin," she said gaily.

At the top of the hill, where the low stone wall under the trees was broken by a weathered, five-barred gate, even Norah paused, however. A new, bright steel padlock and chain challenged them.

" It never used to be even closed," Pixie said anxiously.

" Come on. Easy enough to climb over," Norah told them. " I tell you, I'll explain if we meet anybody—it isn't real trespassing."

But they walked warily, picking their way as though stalking, once they were in the wood. A broad green ride led downhill, into a thick plantation of birches, and beyond, lower still, became mossy and damp under foot, where cedars made a tunnel of flat, dark branches.

" Isn't it cold?" Pixie whispered, shivering.

" And quiet!" Mary put in.

Almost at once, as though to contradict her, jays began screaming somewhere among the high branches a hundred yards ahead.

Norah paused.

" Something's scared them," she warned.

" Us, I expect," Pat suggested.

Norah shook her head.

" No—listen—voices."

They listened, looked at one another and " froze " as they had learned to do when playing stalking games in camp. Even Mary, copying the others, stood stock-still, balancing precariously on a fallen log.

Out of sight, behind a thicket of tangly hazels, people were arguing. Two men's voices, rather gruff, kept speaking in turns, and the shrill, angry talk of an old woman interrupted them. The Marigolds could not make out what the argument was about. Suddenly the woman screamed sharply as though she had been hurt. It was a pathetic scream, very weak and despairing and ended in the most desolate sobs and lamentations.

" That's old Ellie's voice," Norah whispered sharply. " Come on, but don't make a noise."

They crept forward, and presently found themselves looking down into a little hollow, where, on the bank of a winding, narrow stream, a dilapidated hut, built mainly of rusty corrugated iron, stood, surrounded by a broken fence.

A hand-cart on two wheels stood in front of the hut, and two men, whom the girls knew to be Lady Royston's estate workers, were carrying out some poor furniture to pile on it.

Old Ellie, the gipsy, sat on the stump of a tree, her ragged scarlet shawl thrown over her head, rocking herself from side to side and wailing pitifully.

" The beasts!" Norah's face blazed suddenly white. " I believe they're turning that poor old thing out, after all the years and years she's lived here."

The men did not seem to enjoy the task themselves. One, a square built, middle-aged man with grey hair, paused beside the old woman and touched her on the shoulder.

" See here, Mother, don't carry on at us. Orders is orders, you know. Lady Royston said you was to be shifted and shift it's got to be!"

Old Ellie looked up at him in a dazed way. She was small and shrivelled and witch-like, with a face as brown as an Indian's, wispy grey hair and thick, shaggy grey eyebrows, that arched over the blackest eyes imaginable. Her clawlike old hands were clasped on her stick, and shaking, at the moment, with mingled rage and unhappiness.

" Fifty year I've lived here and about—fifty year. If my son Egypt were here he'd not let ye torment me so. It's not long I have to live on the earth and you'd turn me from my freedom and the bit of home I had——"

" Come on now, that's enough." The other man spoke more roughly. He was younger and seemed less patient than his companion. " Why d'you listen to her, Bridges? We've got to do the job—may as well get on with it."

" Stop!"

Norah's voice surprised herself almost as much as it did her patrol. But the sight of anyone in trouble

always roused her, and old Ellie's misery was un-
mistakably genuine. Without waiting to think of
possible consequences, she had crossed the open
space that divided the Marigolds from the little scene
below in a dozen strides and stood facing Bridges and
the other keeper, a flush on her cheeks, her hands
clenched at her sides.

"Stop, I tell you! You can't turn anybody out like
this. It's cruel and mean and—and anyway, Ellie's
never done anybody any harm. Why should she be
turned out?" she ended rather lamely.

The men looked at each other, and the Marigolds,
closing in behind their leader, looked at her. Pat,
trying to whisper something, pulled at her sleeve,
but Norah was in no mood to be interrupted and
pushed her hand away impatiently.

"Well, you see, Miss, it's like this——" the man
Bridges began. "*We* haven't got anything against the
old girl, as you might say. But my Lady's home from
London, and things is all to be altered down here
now. She's given strict orders about this——"

"Lady Royston has, you mean?" Norah's chin
went up. "Is she at the house?"

"Yes, Miss, but——"

"Very well. Don't move another thing out of
Ellie's home until I come back, do you understand?
I'm going to see Lady Royston *now*." Norah turned
away, and put her hand reassuringly over the gipsy's
clasped ones. "Don't worry, Ellie, we won't let you
be turned out like this. I promise."

The old woman peered up at her:

"Why, it's the little lady from the camp," she quavered. "God bless your pretty face, my dearie, but what can a child like you do? Her at the house has a heart like the hard grey flints——"

"So she may have," Norah straightened herself, and her eyes flashed. "But she can't do things like this. Come on, you others. We'll go and call on Lady Royston now. We came out to look for adventures. If I know anything, this is going to be one!"

CHAPTER V

The Adventure of the Little Pigs

" Norah, hi! Norah, wait!"

Patsy, rather out of breath in spite of the fact that she usually counted as champion runner of the whole company, caught up with her leader just as that righteously indignant Guide turned out of the woods into the gravelled drive that led, in a roundabout fashion, to the square, low-built, comfortable white manor of Stone House.

The three younger ones, bunched together and hurrying, were some distance behind, for Norah, when she meant business, waited for nobody. She had scoured up through the woods at a pace that had left them labouring to keep her in sight, and Patsy, taking one look at her set face, saw that no argument any of them could bring forward would serve to dissuade her from her present intention of meeting Lady Royston face to face. Patsy sighed. Ready enough to make the best of things, when necessity arose, she lacked Norah's love of a fight for its own sake. Reason told her that the affairs of Ellie the gipsy had, at present, very little actually to do with the Marigold Patrol, and Lady Royston, if she chose, might quite

excusably request them to mind their own business.
But Norah's lips were smiling, and she was breathing
through her nose, while she stared straight ahead with
bright, resentful eyes. Patsy fell into step beside her,
determined to take half, and if possible the larger
half of the trouble she felt sure they would soon
encounter. Not for nothing had she been Norah's
second ever since the patrol first came into existence.

The drive, turning back on itself, led them by a
bridge across a little ornamental lake, where early
daffodils looked at their reflection in the water, to a
low gate in a hedge of budding sweet briar. The gate
stood open, and beyond it the rose-garden, once the
glory of Stone House, stretched to the walls of the
manor itself, and the wide, shallow steps of the portico.

Someone was at work among the as yet leafless
rose trees—busy pruning with secateurs that went
snip-snap purposefully—someone dressed in serviceable grey tweeds, and with a mop of white hair that
gleamed in the afternoon sun.

"Look out, Norah. That *is* Lady Royston," Patsy
warned, as they paused for a second in the gateway,
and the bent figure straightened itself.

But Norah was looking in a different direction, and
her eyes suddenly widened.

"What in the world? Patsy, will you look at those
pigs now? Rooting in those perfect beds of tulips over
there? *Aroosh!*"

Without warning and without apology she launched
herself into the garden and across it, taking the rose

beds in flying leaps, and uttering at intervals whoops
and yells intended to discourage a large and happy
family of baby pigs who, arrived from heaven knew
where, had, apparently, decided to lay waste entirely
the section of Stone House garden which was given
over to beds of spring bulbs.

" Quick—head them off—turn them back!" Lady
Royston, roused to the situation, abandoned her
pruning and ran to Norah's assistance with an alacrity
surprising in an old lady not far from seventy. " You
over there—shut the gate. Good gracious, they'll
be all over the garden in a moment! Grrr! You little
beast!"

This as a pale pink piglet, squealing with fright,
dodged between her feet and all but sent her sprawling.

The hunting instinct is strong in the most civilized
of us, and a pig hunt, involving no less than fourteen
diminutive, but purposeful, obstinate and panicky
baby pigs can be an exciting undertaking, even for
six human beings. Patsy had joined in before she
knew where she was, and the Marigolds' reinforce-
ments, arrived on the scene, needed no second invitation
to the party.

" Drive them up in the corner of the hedge—all of
them together. We can manage them best that way,"
Lady Royston ordered breathlessly. " Now, two of
you keep them there. I must call the men to carry
them back to the sty. If we try to drive them, they'll
only do more damage."

" We'll carry them." Biddie—never afraid of

animals—grabbed a loudly protesting piglet under each arm, and struggled to her feet again. "Where's their sty, please?"

"Oh, Biddie, how can you?" Pixie shuddered. "They smell horrid."

"Nonsense!" Patsy, also roused to the occasion, followed her sister's example, and Norah, refusing to be outdone, picked up three squirming little objects in her long-armed embrace, and clasping them to her bosom, abjured them to:

"Come along with Nannie now, and it's no good arguing!"

With Lady Royston leading the way, they made a procession round the house, across the tennis lawn and through the kitchen gardens, to the barn and pigsties, where their advent caused considerable consternation to a lad in leggings and a green apron, who had just discovered that the family of a particularly large and unpleasant-looking old black sow had mysteriously vanished.

"I couldn't believe my eyes, M'arm," he told Lady Royston. "I was just thinking——"

"Thinking, were you, William?" Lady Royston snorted wrathfully. "If you did more and thought less, it might be a great deal better for everybody. While you were *thinking* the animals in your charge were digging up the best Darwin tulips, and goodness knows what damage they might have done if we hadn't caught them when we did. Thanks to these—these——" she paused, and for the first time looked

curiously at the Marigolds—" these young ladies,"
she went on firmly, " we rounded up the whole herd
in time. Now, go and call Jennings and fetch the rest
of the pigs from the rose garden."

" Yes, M'am—yes, m'Lady——" William, sub-
dued, went off to do as he was told.

Lady Royston dropped the iron trap-gate of the
sty behind the seventh piglet, and having assured
herself that it really was in position and no more
escapes were likely to take place, took off her gardening
gloves, and very deliberately held out her hand to
Norah.

" I've no idea who you are, nor how you came to
be in my garden with your friends—but I'm exceedingly grateful to you, and as pig-catchers I think you
are all remarkably efficient people," she said briskly.
" Shake hands!"

They shook hands accordingly. Now the excitement was over and they had leisure to observe the
owner of the Stone House, they saw that she was a
pleasant, rather stout old lady, with a hooked nose,
a firm mouth, and very bright, blue eyes under eyebrows that were still dark, though her hair was white
as flax. She wore a shabby, baggy tweed coat and skirt,
that had obviously seen years of hard wear; her big,
clumpy shoes were thick with mud; and there was a
hank of bass sticking out of her pocket. In spite of
all these things she had a very fine dignity about her,
and an air of command that made Pat, who had just
remembered on what errand they had originally come

to the Stone House, quail a little, as the blue eyes rested on her.

" And now," said Lady Royston, " suppose you tell me your names and what business brought you here?"

Before Pat could stammer a reply, Norah swept to the rescue with one of her totally unexpected changes of front.

" I'm afraid," she said disarmingly, " that we were minding much more than our own business when we came—at least, I was. The others just came along with me because they're my patrol. You see, we were really trespassing in your woods, and we saw your keepers turning an old gipsy called Ellie out of her house, and somehow she was so miserable and it seemed so hard, that I thought I'd come and ask you if you knew about it. I thought perhaps you didn't understand *all* about it, you see."

Pat and Biddie held their breath, as Lady Royston frowned alarmingly at their leader.

" You were trespassing, were you? And why, may I ask?"

Norah merely looked thoughtful, and seemed to consider the question.

" Partly because we always used to be allowed to come into these woods in Captain's time, so it's got to be a kind of habit. Partly because we wanted to do something definitely piratical," she said.

" Definitely *what*?" Lady Royston asked.

Norah blinked quickly.

" Piratical—like the pirates," she explained, and

added confidentially. "You see, our school Guide
Company has been suspended because there's no
room for it and it won't start again unless we do something special to ' make good ', so just at the moment
we're sailing under the Jolly Roger—sort of outlaws,
in fact."

"Humph!" Lady Royston snorted. She was still
frowning, but her eyes had begun to twinkle, and her
mouth was not so stern. "I haven't the least idea
what you're talking about, except that I gather you
are Guides—or have been. Well, so am I—or have
been. Come along up to the house. It's four o'clock,
and we're all very thirsty. We'll get to the bottom of
this over a cup of tea."

"But——" for the first time in the course of a
decidedly difficult conversation Norah was at a loss.

"Well—what is it?" Lady Royston asked.

"Only—only old Ellie. I mean, I did promise
her I'd try to get you to let her stay," she stammered.

She did not in the least want to persist with a subject
which, she felt instinctively, might cause Lady Royston's patience to vanish entirely. She felt hot and
thirsty, and, now the excitement was over, definitely
tired from the long walk and the exercise incidental
to the pig hunt. She knew that the other Marigolds,
particularly the two little ones, must be feeling even
more ready for their tea than she was, and besides
she was exceedingly intrigued by Lady Royston. The
old lady attracted her, and she longed to know how and
when she could ever have been a Guide. It needed

a considerable amount of courage to persist, in the face of her own judgment, pleading Ellie's cause.

" Ellie—you mean that old gipsy who has been living in a hovel down by the stream?" Lady Royston inquired. " The place isn't fit for a dog to kennel in. She'll be much better in the alms houses at Dalston."

" She won't—oh, she won't!" Norah's voice rose sharply, and to her own very great annoyance, tears came into her eyes—tears of pity and indignation. " Ellie'll die if you send her to the alms houses. It'll be like prison to her. Gipsies *can't* live in a town. Oh, please listen to me, because I do know. Ellie'd rather live over there, in that pig-sty, than in the alms houses."

" Tut-tut! Don't get so excited, my good girl!" Lady Royston spoke much more kindly than might have been expected. " This is a perfectly free country, and if Ellie, as you call her, doesn't choose to go to Dalston, nobody can force her to. The gipsies have right of tenure in these woods since the sixteenth century, and I can't turn them out, even if I wanted to do it. My keepers told me Ellie would be willing and glad to go."

Norah was resentfully scrubbing her nose with a very clean handkerchief, and Pat, seeing an answer of some sort was expected, came to the rescue.

" Ellie grumbles sometimes," she explained. " Perhaps she did to them. But that's just her way."

Biddie, who had been opening and shutting her

mouth rather like a fish for several minutes, trying to get a word in edgeways, spoke earnestly.

" Lady Royston, have you ever seen old Ellie yourself—really to talk to, I mean?"

" No," Lady Royston admitted.

" I think if you did you'd see what Norah means about her. That's all," she said, steadily.

" Now that's a very sensible suggestion," Lady Royston said heartily. " If I send down word to my keepers to hold their hand until after tea, and then come with you to see this woman, will you be satisfied?"

" Oh, would you? Would you really do that? Oh, you are kind!" Norah exclaimed joyfully.

" Very well. Now find those two children we left in the rose garden and come along. By the time we've washed the pigs off ourselves Miller will have tea ready—and I'm sure we are all more than ready for it!"

CHAPTER VI

Something to Work For

" So you intend to ' make bad '. I see." Lady Royston, pouring out second cups from the big silver tea pot, seemed to be considering the Marigold's avowed intention carefully.

The big, sunny drawing-room at Stone House, with its faded, green and gold panelled walls, its chintz-covered furniture and blazing log-fire was a friendly room. It smelt pleasantly of pot-pourri, and, just now, of hot scones as well. The wide, comfortable arm-chairs and small, fat footstools invited one to curl up complicatedly, or else to hump oneself, knees to chin, in those attitudes which conduce most naturally to confidential and earnest discussion of a patrol's problems.

The Marigolds had disposed of all but the trimmings of a remarkably adequate tea. It had begun with the hot scones and was ending with home-made chocolate cake, and the sort of gingerbread that has a perpetual surprise-packet of almonds, currants or sultanas in every mouthful. Even small Mary Glover had so far expanded out of her shyness as to make two separate remarks without being spoken to, and Pixie would have been talking nineteen to the dozen if Biddie had not firmly snubbed her every time she began. Biddie had the prudent feeling that Lady Royston was much better left to Norah and Pat, at any rate until she knew all there was to be known about the patrol.

Answering her question, Norah said a little doubtfully:

" Well, I don't mean to do anything awful, you know —but ' make good ' we will *not*, in the way Vivian, the head girl I was telling you about, means. It's much too dull and stodgy," and she added, catching Lady Royston's eye and smiling suddenly, " I'm sure you'd have felt the same at our age!"

" Oh, my dear child, what I should have done at your age is quite beside the point!" Lady Royston said hastily—a fraction too hastily.

The patrol were instantly on the alert.

" Did you do awful things, too?" Pixie asked, before anyone could stop her.

Biddie, staring earnestly at the fine old face, said meditatively:

" All really nice people get into rows when they're our age. Daddy was always in rows."

" Tell us what you're thinking about—please do," Norah wheedled shamelessly.

Lady Royston looked across at her and smiled a trifle grimly.

" I was thinking, as a matter of fact, of a day when my dear mother told me that as I should obviously never learn to behave like a lady she hoped I should

do my best to act like a gentleman," she said. " That
was when I had been running wild for a whole summer
with my five brothers, on a farm in Sussex. We
climbed trees, and rode the ploughhorses bare back,
and played at Red Indians—it was a good time."

" Red Indians—did *you* like playing Red Indians?"
Mary asked breathlessly.

Pixie, screwing up her face, said curiously:

" I don't see what your mother meant. How could
you be a gentleman?"

" Don't be silly, Pixie," Norah admonished kindly,
" she meant be brave and honourable and straight,
even if you couldn't put on airs and graces, didn't
she, Lady Royston?"

The old lady nodded.

" Yes—that's right. I've often remembered her
words since, for airs and graces, as you call them, have
never been much in my line."

" Or in ours!" Pat said emphatically. She added,
after a pause, " I suppose you weren't a Guide then,
were you?"

" Good gracious, no. You seem to forget that I'm
a very old woman! Guides hadn't been invented when
I was a very young girl, I'm afraid. You girls don't
know how lucky you are, with so many things you can
do. One had to do something."

The Marigolds stared at the fire. They had all
noticed, as they came through the oak-panelled hall,
the picture of a boy in flying kit, with a wreath of
laurel hanging beneath it.

Lady Royston went on smoothly:

" I was one of the original Guide Officers Association Training School—one of Mrs. Blythe's ' Goats ', as they called us. After that I worked for years as a Commissioner in the Docks."

" What are you now?" Biddie asked anxiously.

" Nothing at the moment. My daughter married a Hungarian diplomat, and years ago I went out to stay in Hungary for a time. I gave up Guiding then. But——" she looked them over quizzically, " I haven't forgotten all about it, yet."

Biddie bent forward, and stared at her earnestly.

" Do you think it was fair of Miss Nesbitt to suspend our company?" she asked.

Lady Royston ignored the murmur of expostulation from Norah and Pat, as she said cheerfully:

" Fair or not fair, it needn't do you much harm, unless you let it. Tell me some more about your plans for ' making bad '."

" Well, as a matter of fact," Norah owned, " we haven't got many yet. We meant to have a Patrol Council this afternoon, but——" she spread out her hands expressively.

" What with rescuing gipsies and hunting baby pigs there hasn't been a lot of time," Lady Royston ended the sentence for her. " Well, now—what do you want to do? Scatter a box of tin tacks in a car park, or burgle the Bank of England, or what?"

" Oh, no!" Norah's face crinkled into delighted denial. " We don't want to do those sort of bad things at all. We want to be Guides just as much as ever. You know, help other people at all times and that sort of thing. But we want to make an adventure of it, instead of being dull and stuck and goody-goody. D'you see at all what I mean?"

Lady Royston nodded. The sun had slipped down behind the trees on the edge of the park and shadows were beginning to come out of the corners of the room and dance on the ceiling in the fire-light. When she spoke again her voice was deep, and thrilled through the quiet room:

" Merchant adventurers, chaunting at the windlass.
　Early in the morning, we slipped from Plymouth Sound.
　All for Adventure in the great New Regions,
　All for Eldorado and to sail the world around.
　Sing!　The red of sun-rise ripples round the bows
　　　again.
　Merchant adventurers, oh, sing, we're outward bound.
　All to stuff the sunset in our old black galleon,
　All to seek the merchandise that no man ever found."

She broke off, and asked, smiling a little, " Is that how you feel about things?"

" Yes—oh yes!" Norah sat forward in the big armchair, her hands clasped tight, her eyes shining. " Oh, do go on—please!"

But Lady Royston shook her head.

" Not now. This isn't the moment to be quoting poetry. We've to go and see your old Ellie before it gets dark. Now, listen to me, you Marigold Patrol, or Pirate Crew, or whatever you are—I've been thinking while we talked. I've something to suggest to you."

They nodded, staring at her gravely, and a little bit anxiously. They had only known Lady Royston a very short time, but when she spoke in just that way they felt instinctively that something important was coming.

" You're tired of playing at Guiding, and doing ordinary, hum-drum good-turns, you say? Very well. You came up here this afternoon to interfere in business that didn't concern you. Norah admitted as much frankly. People who mind more than their own business must be prepared to take the responsibility. I have decided to let old Ellie stay where she is for the present. But she can't live in that hut through another winter. Now, you may come and go where you like on the estate from now until next October. You are welcome to visit me any Saturday afternoon, between two and six, and ask me to instruct you in any Guide subject I know anything about—*but*——" Lady Royston paused.

" But what?" Norah breathed.

" But if Ellie the gipsy hasn't either a hut or a cottage that's fit for a human being to live in by the last day of October this year, into the alms house at Dalston she shall go—and *I'm* not going to lift a finger to prevent it," Lady Royston promised them gravely.

" You mean—you mean that *we* must see she has a proper place to live in—we, all by ourselves?" Pat asked incredulously. "But how can we? We can't build houses and we haven't any money and——"

Norah stood up abruptly. Her eyes were shining:

"We haven't anything—but we'll do it!" she said exultantly. "Lady Royston, you're a brick, and you understand things better than anybody ever has. I don't know how in the world we shall do this thing, but I know we can—and we'll do it or bust!"

CHAPTER VII

A Plan of Campaign

" Lady Royston's nice, and I like her a lot, but the more I think about her, the more sure I am that she's quite, quite mad."

Pat, exploding out of the cloak-room at St. Bridget's, like a bullet out of a gun in her anxiety not to waste a moment of the twenty minutes mid-morning recreation on Monday, addressed her patrol leader without preamble.

Norah, with studied unconcern, bent to tie her shoe lace.

" Do you think so?" she asked politely.

" Oh, don't be silly, Norah. You know as well as I do that we can't—just can't possibly—make any sort of kind of a house—not even a hut—fit for anybody to live in. I mean—well, how can we?"

Norah rubbed her nose thoughtfully, without replying. They began to stroll up and down the gravel path that bordered the tennis lawns behind the school. Fifty or sixty other girls were doing the same thing, but they were both much too absorbed to notice any interruption. On the far side of the brick wall at the end of the courts, they could hear the juniors, also taking recreation time.

Pat shook her head.

" Us!" she said with scorn.   " Why, Norah, a whole company couldn't do such a thing. It'd cost pounds and pounds to get the materials, even if we did the building ourselves."

" Mm—I know." Norah nodded. Then she did a funny little double shuffle of excitement. " Wouldn't it be jolly though? A real thatched cottage, Pat—with two rooms and a proper fireplace, and a crooked chimney. We'd have to buy Ellie a black cat and one of those garden-brooms made of twigs, and she could set up in business as a witch straight away."

" Oh, of course, if you're going to be absolutely daft——" Pat remarked despairingly.

" No, I'm not, Pat, really I'm not. It's only that my mind works a funny way round. I always have to see a thing very hard, if I'm going to have a job in getting it. Then I mind enough about it to work and work and work until it comes true. I've been thinking about Ellie's home all the week-end and I've really got some quite sensible ideas."

" Then for goodness' sake let's hear them," Pat demanded anxiously. " The bell will go before we've made any plans if you don't hurry."

" Well, listen. To begin with we just must find out something about buildings, and how much wood and bricks and things cost and how one starts building a house. The only way I can think of is to go up to Ringan's estate where they're putting up all those little new houses, and watch the men working. Maybe

we could talk to some of them, if they looked nice—
and even if we didn't do that, we could notice the
names and addresses on the carts that bring the bricks
and materials. Then we'd be further on than we are
now, anyway," she added a little defiantly. Pat did
not look terribly enthusiastic.

After a few minutes silence she sighed.

"I almost wish we hadn't got to bother about
this," she said unhappily. "It isn't that I don't
want to help Ellie. I do. But it's going to be so awfully
difficult that it seems to me it'll take every bit of time
we ever have, and we shan't be able to get on with
any of the things we were planning to do."

"Oh, I don't know," Norah refused to be down-
cast. "After all, Lady Royston said she'd help us
with Guide things whenever we asked her, and besides,
Pat, this really is doing something *with* Guide training.
Finding out about an entirely new subject beats Kim's
game as an observation test, every time, if you ask
me."

"That's true!" Pat laughed. "Isn't there something about judging quantities in first class, too? We'll
certainly be learning our work practically, which was
what Captain used to say mattered. When are you
going up to Ringan's?"

"This evening, directly after tea. Come with me?"

"Rather. What about the kids?"

"Better leave them out on this, hadn't we? I don't
think a crowd of us standing staring would be a good
idea, besides, we don't need them. Let's tell them to

find out all they can for themselves, and bring their ideas to a patrol meeting on Wednesday."

" Right. I'll tell Biddie as we go in now. I can get permission to speak to her for a minute on the stairs. I don't suppose they'll produce a practical notion between the three of 'em, but still——"

" Does them good to try, anyway," Norah said cheerfully. " I don't believe in having a patrol and doing all the work for them. Too much of that in most companies these days. There's the bell. Tell Biddie what we want them to find out is how much it costs to build a house, and then how we can make enough money to do it, and that the one who brings the most sensible answer can choose where we go next time we are having a Saturday hike."

.   .   .   .

Somewhat to Norah's surprise, she found Biddie instead of Pat waiting for her outside the gate at five o'clock that evening.

" Pat got nabbed for her extra music lesson," the younger sister explained. " Miss Powell rang Mummie up while we were at afternoon school, and asked if Pat could change her time, and Mummie said yes. Pat's absolutely wild!"

" She needn't be—there'll be plenty of other times to go up to Ringan's," Norah said placidly.

" Oh," Biddie looked crestfallen. " Can't I go with you, Norah? Pat told me what you're going to do, and I think it sounds fun".

Norah appeared to consider.

" Hadn't you any scheme of your own?" she inquired.

" Not really. Mary's going to the public library, to read books about building, and Pixie thought p'raps the man at the Estate Agents in Nelson Street could tell us things. The only idea I had was to write to ' Robin Hood ' who runs the League of Young Adventure in the *Daily Mercury*. He *says* he'll send answers to *any* question, if you remember to put a $1\frac{1}{2}d$. stamp in your letter when you write to him."

Norah looked at Biddie's serious face and chuckled.

" Been trying to think it out for yourselves, haven't you?" she commented. " Well, provided you write your letter after you get home, Biddie, you're welcome to come along with me if you want to. It's a jolly walk up to Ringan's, anyway, on an evening like this."

They fell into step together. Norah, slight, springy, taking long easy strides, and Biddie plodding beside her, very square-shouldered, solid and dependable. On the outskirts of the town, almond trees were in bloom, and early lilac in bud. Norah paused more than once to stare up at the fragile pink stars of the almond flowers, standing out against the pale March sky, or to crane her neck over some hedge beyond which she could catch a glimpse of crocuses, spilling their royal purple and gold in the wayside gardens. Dropping from her tip-toes, after one such effort, she caught Biddie's eye, and flushed a little.

" This time of year drives me a bit mad, I think," she confided apologetically to the younger Guide.

" I'm always so thrilled to see things growing again—I can't ever take flowers for granted, just because they come back every year, can you? It always seems like a sort of miracle when they begin coming out again."

Biddie nodded whole-heartedly.

" I feel like that too—only I'm not much good at talking about things, ever," she admitted, and added rather abruptly: " You know, Norah, it's that sort of feeling that made me so sorry for old Ellie. If you'd lived out of doors all your life, it'd be bound to be worse shut up in a town house in spring than any other time of the year."

Norah agreed. It surprised her a little to find that Biddie had enough imagination to realize such a factor in the case of old Ellie. Perhaps being in the same patrol as her elder sister suppressed her in the ordinary way. Norah decided she must try to get to know Biddie better.

They began, quite naturally, to talk about gardens, and after a few minutes, Biddie said rather diffidently:

" You know, Norah, I expect we could make a lovely herb garden, if we asked old Ellie to help us. Gipsies know just all there is to be known about herbs, and if we took roots and seeds out of the woods we could cultivate them, and then make lots of remedies, like the Red Indians do."

Norah stopped stock still a moment and stared at her companion.

" Why—what's the matter?" Biddie asked, flushing behind her freckles.

"Nothing—only that red hair sometimes thatches a remarkable set of brains, my child," Norah told her. "That's an absolute inspiration, if you ask me. Don't you *see*, we can get old Ellie to grow her own herbs in a garden round her house, and then maybe she can sell them, or maybe we can. I'm sure lots of people would be glad of remedies to cure colds and headaches and chilblains and that sort of silly things that aren't really being ill, but make you feel horrid. And then we could make pot-pourri—the kind they sell at the herb shops in London. My aunt sent me a box once and it smelt gorgeous. Oh, Biddie, I'm certain there's lots and lots in the idea. Ellie could almost make her own living by it, if we managed properly."

"I hadn't thought of anything so sort of elaborate as that," Biddie protested, rather anxiously. "I was thinking we could beg a patch of the garden at home and just experiment a bit, that was all."

"We'll see," Norah promised. "Anyway, it's an idea to put to the patrol. Nobody can say the Marigolds stick in a rut, anyway! Come on—we'll take the short cut this way—it'll save us time."

As she spoke, Norah dived into a narrow cinder alley, which led between the fences of a number of big, old fashioned houses, and a stretch of open ground that was being cultivated as allotments. At the far end of the alley, skeleton roofs against the sky proclaimed the building the two had come to watch.

CHAPTER VIII

Mr. Hewlett changes his Mind

" What a perfectly hateful, cross, stupid old man!"

Biddie, red as a turkey-cock, and stuttering, looked back over her shoulder at the group of grinning workmen outside one of the unfinished houses, and if looks could kill there would have been an instant and wholesale slaughter. Norah, her hands in her pockets, did not turn, but she, too, was angry—very angry.

" Ordering us off as if we were tramps or—or—oh, I think people are perfectly horrid!" Biddie continued to complain.

" Well, I suppose he was tired—it's the end of the day. Maybe it was a silly idea of mine that we could make friends with people by watching them work. But he needn't have been so cross and rude——"

Norah, struggling to be just, felt it hard to make allowances for the little, fat, elderly man, in shirt sleeves and a bowler hat, who had suddenly appeared on the scene, just when she was beginning to get thoroughly interested in watching the work. She and Biddie had struck up an acquaintance with a pleasant-faced boy, who was rather leisurely sawing up wood in the entrance to a house which had got as far as having walls, though it had no roof. He had begun to explain to them most obligingly just how foundations had to be dug, when the old man bounced down the half-finished stairs and began to grumble and complain.

" There you go again, Jim, always gossiping to someone. You men are kept on overtime to get this job through quickly, and look at you. Do you imagine these houses are going to grow up themselves, while you tell fairy tales to a pack of idle little schoolgirls? Be off, you two—be off! I don't want to hear a word you've got to say."

Norah, whose ready Irish tongue had got her out of so many scrapes in the past that she was beginning to trust to it, tried to explain their presence, but the little old man refused to listen. He was comically red in the face with annoyance, and flapped his arms at them as though they were a couple of chickens he wished to shoo out into the road.

" Guides—Guides, are you? Well, just guide yourselves out of here, and double quick at that!" he had advised them. " I've been plagued enough with idle tykes of children for this day!"

Jim, looking shamefaced, tried to make excuse: " I was only telling them, Mr. Hewlett, sir——"

But Mr. Hewlett would not be mollified. The only thing Norah and Pat could do was to walk away, with as much dignity as they could summon, and even so, they found themselves heading for the road and the longest way home, too much ruffled to realize it before a change of purpose meant running the gauntlet of the other workmen, who evidently considered Jim's and their discomfiture most amusing.

"Oh, well, we're getting exercise, if nothing else!" Norah groaned. "I hope the others are doing better than we've done, Biddie, or we shan't get far at the next Patrol Council!"

"Well, I did look hard at that man laying bricks, and it seemed to me fairly easy." Biddie tried to be cheerful. "He put them sort of alternately, so as a whole one came over a crack—did you see?"

"One plain, one purl, next row one purl, one plain," Norah agreed flippantly. "Yes—and they don't dig big foundations nowadays—only what that boy called 'footings', so that's one comfort. I didn't see how we could possibly hunk out real deep foundations in the wood, 'cos of all the tree roots. It's one of the things that's been worrying me."

"I say," Biddie suggested. "It's quite early still. Now we've got on to the road, instead of going the short cut, shall we walk down and meet Pat? She'll only just be out of school and she was so bored at having to go."

"That's an idea. Let's!" Norah hastened her pace a little as they swung down the long hill together, into the town, keeping step, but saying little. Both were deep in thought. Dusk was falling—the lilac-coloured dusk of early March. A few cars had already switched on their lights, which dazzled like great yellow flowers. The rush of evening traffic had begun along the high road at the bottom of the hill, and the traffic signals stabbed the twilight—red—amber—green—red. Watching them, Norah frowned.

" I say, Biddie, that light's changing in a funny way, isn't it? Something's gone wrong with the automatic switch, I believe. Amber only shows between red and green—green's changing to red without warning."

Biddie screwed up her eyes.

" I don't know—is it? Or are we just imagining it?" she murmured, her mind evidently running in another channel.

They counted carefully, and by the time they had reached the kerb, were convinced.

" It's doing it both sides of the road the same. I say, you know, that's jolly dangerous," Biddie said anxiously.

Almost before the words were out of her mouth, the thing had happened. The light showing up the hill changed without warning from green " go " to red " stop ". A car's brakes squealed, and an old-fashioned two-seater skidded to a stop well over the white line of the pedestrian crossing. At the same time a bike shot out from behind it. The school-boy riding the bike saw, a second too late, the light against him. With a white, scared face, he swerved his front wheel in to the left too quickly and came off in a heap. Not much harm would have been done. Small boys fall proverbially lightly. But to their horror Biddie and Norah realized he was not alone on the bicycle. In the flash of time as he rounded the

3

car they caught a glimpse of the little bundle in pale blue astraddle on the bar, clutching the handles with obvious delight. As the bike went over, the child—not more than three years old—was pitched clear over the front, far beyond the warning danger line into the very path of the main road traffic.

It all happened so quickly that passers-by hardly saw there was an emergency, and Biddie could never afterwards explain exactly what happened. She only knew that before she could gather her scattered wits, Norah had darted off the kerb, grabbed the little bundle up into her arms in some fashion and then a car—a big, grey, streamline sports—was between them —had passed, and Norah was back beside her, something queer about her face, about the way she was smiling.

" She's all right—nothing touched her—she's just bumped her knees a bit, I expect!" she panted, as she handed over the now screaming child to the boy, obviously an elder brother, who looked ready to faint with shock.

The child—a pretty little girl with black curls—was smothered in dust, and the knees of her leggings were torn, but Biddie guessed from the hearty way she was yelling, the damage she had sustained was not serious. She had soon investigated the extent of it, and, drawing a bandage from her pocket, proceeded to tie up a couple of grazes.

" She's not a bit badly hurt. I should take her home at once, now she's stopped crying," she advised the brother kindly. Just then Norah clutched her arm.

" Come away—quick," she whispered urgently. " There's going to be a crowd here in a minute."

Dragging Biddie with her, she turned into the main road, then, before Biddie could protest, dived up a quiet side turning, and leaned against the railings of an empty house. They had only come about a hundred yards, but Biddie had had time to notice she was clutching her left arm.

" Norah—you're hurt," she exclaimed, anxiously.

Norah nodded, white to the lips.

" Don't make a fuss. It's my elbow—the mud-guard on that car caught it as I turned round. It's all right, Biddie—just—I always hate being hit on the funny bone!"

" Here—sit down on the step and put your head between your knees. You'll faint if you don't." Gently Biddie forced her leader to obey. " Let me look at your arm."

Norah, in spite of herself, winced away.

" I'd—rather you didn't," she said shakily.

Biddie looked very grave.

" I won't hurt," she promised.

Her strong, square hands, with their short, stubby fingers were most unexpectedly gentle, as she peeled back Norah's sleeve, and exposed the elbow, where a deep and angry bruise was already beginning to show on each side of a considerable gash.

" Thank goodness it's not broken!" she said, after a minute's careful examination.

Norah raised her head from her knees.

" However do you know?" she asked.

" Keep quiet and don't talk," Biddie ordered, with quaint authority. " I often help Daddie in his surgery. Of course I know."

The road had been deserted, but just then a car turned into it and stopped beside them. Annoyed, Biddie looked up and recognized it as the shabby tourer that had been on the scene of the accident. The driver got out, and she caught her breath in surprise. He was a little fat man, in black clothes and a bowler hat—the foreman of the builders up at Radletts, whom Jim had called " Mr. Hewlett ".

He came straight over to them, and Biddie saw his expression was now one of sincere concern.

" Is the young lady hurt? My word, that was a plucky risk you took, Miss, if you'll excuse me for saying so! I wager that little girl owes her life to you, and the lad maybe more'n his life, seeing how he'd have felt, if he'd seen her run over before his eyes. Oh, my goodness, what a nasty, crool cut you've got there! Still, it might have been worse. Come and sit down in the car, my dear, while we bind it up, and then, maybe, I can take you home—if you'll allow me the privilege."

Norah and Biddie could hardly believe their ears. This was a very different person from the Mr. Hewlett who had been so rude to them at Radletts! However, they were both rather badly shaken up, and only too glad to agree to his suggestion.

As he settled Norah comfortably on the worn seat, the springs of which left much to be desired, Biddie produced her second bandage and set to work with it and a clean handkerchief in a businesslike fashion that seemed to astonish him considerably.

" I never did! Quite a little nurse, aren't you, my dear? You modern young ladies certainly do seem to know how to deal with emergencies." He paused, looking at them more closely, then said slowly: " Am I making a mistake, Miss—was you two speaking to young Jim Willox up on the buildings 'bout half an hour ago?"

" We were talking to a boy who was sawing up wood. *You* came and ordered us off," Norah said bluntly.

" It didn't matter. If you hadn't we shouldn't have come home this long way round, and maybe then that baby would have been killed," Biddie put in philosophically.

Mr. Hewlett shook his head several times then he pushed back his bowler and scratched it, as though hopeful that might produce an idea. Finally he said:

" Well, I'm sorry. I thought you was the sort as comes hanging around, wasting my men's time with idle questions. Now I see—well—maybe there was something you *did* want to know about?"

Norah, nursing an arm that thanks to Biddie was paining her considerably less, chuckled.

" Just one or two things, Mr. Hewlett," she said happily. " Just one or two, when you can spare us the time!"

CHAPTER IX

A Bargain is Struck

" Well, I don't know how you feel about it, but for myself I'd say this has been a properly elastic-sided week!"

Norah, swinging her long legs from the lowest branch of the beech tree, just inside the upper gate of Royston Park, bit well into an apple, and spat out the stem with unladylike precision.

" A *what* sort of a week?" Pat inquired, bending at a perilous angle out of the branch above to try and get a sight of her leader's face. Norah waved her apple in a gesture of explanation.

" You know—elastic-sided—expanding. Sometimes Saturday seems to come next door to Monday in a week—other times there's a month between the two. It feels ages and ages since we came here last Saturday, that's what I'm getting at."

" You'll be getting at a broken neck in a minute if you don't look out," Biddie warned her from below. " Do be careful with your arm in a sling—you look awfully as if you might overbalance up there."

" Don't fuss, child," Norah ordered cheerfully. " I'm only wearing this beastly sling to please you anyway. But listen, my infants, if you've all finished lunch, let's get on down to Ellie's. Lady Royston's expecting us at three and we want plenty of time for our first visit, don't we? Mary, have you had enough to eat—really?"

Mary, sitting cross-legged on her mackintosh, like a small frog on a lily-leaf, nodded solemnly.

" Heaps and heaps, but truly you shouldn't all——"

" Nonsense!" Pat cut her short, swinging herself down from her perch, as she spoke. " If a patrol can't feed its recruits now and again on the spur of the moment what's the use of saying its motto is ' Be Prepared '? But I very much hope the odd assortment of spare parts you've just consumed agrees—if you think you're going to die at any moment let us know, won't you?"

Mary grinned.

" I don't feel a bit like dying yet," she announced calmly.

" Odd little beast, isn't she?" Pat remarked to Norah pityingly, as they walked on ahead of the rest down the green ride to Ellie's cottage. " Fancy coming off like that for the day out without a thing in the way of provisions. D'you think she's properly looked after by those people she lodges with?"

" No, I certainly do not," Norah said grimly. " You heard what she said—that she ' quite often ' doesn't get anything to eat from breakfast until tea time, so the fact they wouldn't give her anything to bring with her didn't seem to matter? I wonder if her mother knows how she's treated?"

Pat shrugged.

" She seems to me the sort of kid who never would squeal, so quite probably her mother hasn't the least idea. It seems pretty awful, doesn't it?"

Norah nodded.

" I'm only so glad she came along to us. We can look after her and help her a bit, if we aren't too obvious about it. Mummie'll always make me up an extra dinner for her, when we go out hiking and things like that. She's an asset in the patrol, too. Have you noticed how young Pixie's begun to open her eyes and take notice of her blessings lately?"

Pat grinned her assent.

" Biddie said only yesterday she was never going to grouse about us being hard up at home again," she remarked, " because we had got each other and Mummie and Daddie, and a house that we all belonged in, instead of having to lodge alone with strangers. I guessed then she must have been talking to Mary."

" Long live the Chiefs! Belonging to a family of a million certainly tends to broaden one's outlook!" Norah reflected cheerfully. " Look, there's Ellie, down by the stream. I wonder if she's going to be in a good temper this afternoon so that we can really talk things over with her? She was so on her guard with Lady Royston last week I didn't feel we got anywhere much, did you?"

Alone with the Marigolds, however, the old gipsy showed every sign of friendliness and gratitude.

" Blessings on your pretty young faces, my lovely

dears, the sun certainly is shining in the wood when I see you all around me, and me the poor person that'd be in a weary little room in a great place no better than a prison, if it wasn't for your kind hearts. And what's this? A present of tea and a packet of tobacco for the poor old gipsy? Dordi, dordi, how can I say thank you enough, now?"

" We don't want any thanks, Ellie, but if you aren't busy we'd like to talk to you a bit," Norah suggested. " You see, there are some things we'd like to discuss with you, and then, besides that, we want to ask you some questions, if you don't mind, questions about herbs," she added quickly, for she remembered reading that gipsies are very shy and loath to be asked about their own affairs.

Ellie pushed back the shawl from her head and her wild, dark eyes swept the faces of the patrol, coming to rest on Biddie.

" There's the one that's asking that question," she said keenly. As Biddie flushed, she held out a clawlike hand. " Turn over your hands, pretty dear. On the inner side of the palms, at the root of each little finger, are three straight lines, uneven-long—am I dukkerin right?"

Interestedly Biddie peered into her own rather grubby palms, and the patrol craned their necks to see if Ellie was romancing.

" It's quite true—but everybody has, haven't they?" Biddie asked.

" I haven't," Norah said.

" Nor have I," Pixie piped up.

"What does it mean, Ellie?" Pat asked curiously.

" Surely, that's the tatchi sign of a healer, the
' stigmata ' of the healer, as they call it. A pretty
nurse you'll make, dearie, or a clever doctor, maybe,
for I hear the young ladies can go for the doctoring
nowadays."

" You're quite right, Ellie, she's splendid at nursing,"
Norah broke in, anxious to humour the old woman.
" She bound up my bad arm beautifully when I hurt
it last week."

" Aye, Ellie saw you'd come by a bad arm, my lady
dear—wait now—come over and sit down for a while.
If we're to have a talk together let's all be comfortable."

She led the way to a giant cedar, growing a little
way behind her dilapidated hut. Its flat green branches
hung out across the stream, and its dry, twisted roots,
pushing up out of the earth, turned the brown bank
into a series of comfortable natural armchairs. When
they were settled there, Ellie insisted on hearing just
how Norah had come by her hurt arm, and finally
induced her to take off the bandage and show her the
wound.

" It's a bit stiff to-day, and sort of hot, I'd rather
you didn't touch it, if you don't awfully mind," she
told the old woman apologetically. She did not want
to wince with the pain, when Mary and Pixie were
looking on.

Ellie peered keenly at the place. " 'Tis an ugly
hurt. It's gotten the drab—the poison, as you say—in

it, that has, dearie. 'Twas cut with a raw, jaggetty piece of metal, you can see, and that's not a natural thing, it isn't like clean steel, nor yet wood, nor a burn. You need the tacheno herbs—there's tacheno herbs for every hurt and every ache and every pain. Wait, now. Are you going up along to the great house, and coming down by this way, in an hour or so? You are that? Then Ellie'll put you a poultice of the witch elm chips on that, to cool it, and when you come back, she'll give you an ointment of marshmallow, with maybe just a touch of Ladies' Slipper root, that'll take the pain out, and heal it clean over, in two or three days —better than doctor's stuff, the tacheno herbs are."

" What sort of herbs?" Biddie asked interestedly.

" Oh, tacheno—that's just a word the poor people use—it means the right ones—the proper sort," old Ellie told them. She added, reflectively: " There's tacheno herbs for every ache and every pain. A poultice of witch elm chips, now—that draws poison —or the marshmallow ointment, with a touch of the Lady Slipper root whiles the pain out. There's not an ill that Ellie can't tell you the tacheno herbs for, lady dear."

Norah thought she was not anxious to be questioned further—it was as though she had let the word slip by accident and was rather annoyed with herself.

On the excuse of fetching things from her hut, she led Norah away from the others, and presently dived into the remote recesses of the dark little place. Waiting in the doorway, Norah had a chance to see just how dilapidated it really was. The walls were crumbling, and light showed between the beams of the roof. It smelt damp and stuffy, but now she could really look inside she did not think it looked as dirty as she had expected. Presently old Ellie came hobbling out with a little tin pannikin full of some brownish-yellow liquid, and a handful of what looked like old sponge, but was actually a tuft of dried Irish moss. Wondering what in the world her mother would say to such a proceeding, Norah let the gipsy soak the moss pad in the liquid and then bind it firmly over her arm, with her hard, skilful old fingers. As the bandage was knotted into place she looked up in surprise.

" Ooh, Ellie, it is lovely and cool!" she said in surprise.

The gipsy cackled with laughter.

" That it is, lady dear—and are you surprised the poor people's remedies is so instant-quick in their working? Aye, there's many a fine doctor in London town would be glad to know all I knows. But Ellie keeps her herbs for them as don't despise them, and for friends she has that bring her kindness and the good heart."

" That reminds me, Ellie." Norah, who was not too sure about Ellie's remedies, took the chance to change the subject. " We didn't come down here to ask you about my arm, really. We wanted to talk to you about the future."

" A'ko?" Ellie gave the typical gipsy grunt, which,

like the Red Indian " *Ugh* " serves to express any number of meanings.

" Yes." Norah drew a deep breath. " You see, Ellie, Lady Royston's a bit—well, you know, fussy about things. I expect that—that house of yours is all right really, but she seems to think it isn't in an awfully good state, and as she explained last Saturday, she wants you to have a new one before next winter."

Ellie stroked her chin, but said nothing. Norah floundered on.

" We'd like to help, in fact, we're *going* to, whatever happens; only we don't want to do it interferingly. I mean, it's going to be your home, so it wouldn't be much sense to plan building it a way you didn't like, would it? What we want you to tell us is, if you've got to have a new house, would the same sort of size and shape as that one over there suit you best, and would you like it built just where that one is, or somewhere different or—or what?"

Ellie's piercing dark eyes considered Norah for a moment, then swept over the serious faces of the rest of the patrol.

" Why are you concerning yourselves for the gipsy person?" she asked suddenly and harshly. " Ellie can't pay for a new fine house, my dears."

" We know that—we quite understand," Pat said quickly, flushing as she spoke.

Norah laughed.

" We're standing the racket, Ellie," she told her. " We don't know yet how, but there's always a way to do things, if you really want to, it seems to me. And," she added in a matter of fact tone, " you can always pay us back by teaching us things, can't you? As Guides, we want to get *at home* in the woods and out-door places, and you can help us to that better than anybody could. You can give us the freedom of the woods, Ellie, in exchange for a little house."

Ellie said nothing. With her head bent, leaning on her stick, she looked more than ever like an old witch, considering a spell. At last she raised her head and said slowly:

" There's things that I knows of the plants and the herbs, aye, and of the birds and the beasts, too. Sure as my own name's Truffeni Leigh (though the folk here abouts call me Ellie) I'll give you measure for measure, my dears, if it's a bargain struck between us. Charity I'm loath to take of Gentile people or Romanies, but a bargain is a bargain. What I knows, that I'll teach, and come the summer-end you'll be as wise as the gipsy folk, that knows more than Gentile people think upon, though they are only poor, tramping beggar men and women. And old Ellie shall have a little house, with a tight roof and a chimney, down by the stream, on the grass plot, there, that's dry and even. Do you shake hands to the bargain?"

" We do!" the Marigolds exclaimed, all together; and solemnly, nodding and smiling at them, Ellie shook hands with each in turn, including small Mary, who stood up very stiff and serious and squinted solemnly through glasses that had slipped down her nose.

CHAPTER X

Stop, Thief!

" My dears, I'm very worried this afternoon—very worried indeed!"

Lady Royston met the patrol at the front door of Stone House, an agitated expression on her face, her manner distraught.

" I am so sorry. Can't we help?" Norah asked anxiously.

" Come in—come in here. Yes, I'm hoping you can."

Mysteriously, Lady Royston led them into the drawing-room and shut the door. Then she looked round anxiously and sinking her voice almost to a whisper, said:

" There's been a burglary."

" What—here?" Pat asked.

Lady Royston nodded.

" Within the last hour. All the old silver from the dining-room sideboard has disappeared."

" But—are you *sure*?" Norah said curiously.

" Certain. It was there when I had my lunch, and when I went back just now, it had gone. While I was in the garden, I noticed a dirty-looking man in

a red pullover, with a sack on his back, and a dog with
him, go across the bridge into the woods.   I noticed
him particularly, because the poor dog was lame, and
trotted along, close in his tracks.   He had been
begging at the back door, cook says, and she'd sent
him away."

The Marigolds looked at each other and then at
their leader.   Norah was gazing straight ahead of her,
with a faint smile twitching the corners of her lips
and her eyes narrowed.

" I say, oughtn't we to ring up the police?" Pixie
shrilled excitedly.

" Oh, Norah, don't let's—let's solve it ourselves,"
Mary chipped in eagerly.

" What do you feel about it, Lady Royston?   Do
you think it's time to call up the police—or not?" Norah
asked.   For a fraction of a second Lady Royston's left
eyelid touched her cheek.

" I'd like you to have a look at the dining-room first
and see what you make of it," she said soberly.   " After
all, I've no great faith in local policemen."

" Right!" Norah turned to her patrol.   " Pat, take
Pixie and go round to the dining-room window—look
carefully to see if you can find any tracks of a person
getting in.   Biddie, if Lady Royston will allow you
to, go and ask cook politely just exactly what happened
about the tramp in the red pullover.   Mary, come
with me, and use your eyes, but don't touch a thing
—not a *thing*, mind you, in the dining-room. We don't
want to confuse any finger-prints the thief may have

been good enough to leave behind. Oh, and Mary, have you got a notebook and pencil? We may need them."

As Lady Royston stood aside to let them file out, her face was completely non-committal, but the worried expression seemed to have vanished as if by magic. Closing the door behind them, she picked up her knitting and sat down in the comfortable armchair by the open window.

" Now, that *ought* to take them quite a time to put together, if they don't miss any of the clues," she said happily to herself. " I will say for them, they're on the spot! I haven't laid a trail for ten years, and it's certainly very interesting to see a new generation at work—if that red-haired patrol leader believes there's been a genuine burglary I'll eat my Sunday hat!"

Norah did *not* believe anything of the kind, and neither did Pat once she had discovered the thread of ravelled scarlet wool sticking just a fraction too obviously to the rose bush under the dining-room window, or Biddie, after two words with grinning, but well prepared cook. Pixie and Mary, however, palpitated with suppressed excitement, speaking in solemn whispers, and staring about them until their eyes nearly fell out of their heads.

" Cook says she gave the man a packet of stale toast-crusts for his dog, and because he said he'd got a bad cold, she gave him a raw onion," Biddie reported, with a perfectly straight face, " and she says he didn't appear to have anything much in his sack, except that a little soot ran out on the white kitchen step, where he'd stood it."

Mary, scribbling feverishly, noted "crusts", "onion" and "soot", after "red jersey" and "lame dog", then looked up for further orders, licking her pencil with an industrious tongue, meanwhile.

"Well, if there aren't enough clues there——" Norah shrugged expressively, eyeing the dining-room meanwhile through narrowed lids. Something by the far end of the sideboard attracted her attention. She sauntered over and picked it up—looked at it a moment, smelt it, then said sharply:

"Biddie, did you ask cook if anyone else called between now and lunch time?"

Biddie nodded.

"I did."

"One up to you!" Norah approved.

"She said a young lady came to the front door to ask something about a subscription for a missionary society."

"Did she let her in?"

"No—spoke to her on the doorstep."

"What was she like?"

"Pretty and well dressed, but rather nervous, driving her own car."

"An Austin twelve?"

"I don't know—a blue car."

"Number ZOG 535—now I wonder why she came in here, exactly?" Norah mused.

The Marigolds crowded round as she spread a

scrap of paper on the table. It was a printed garage receipt for housing a Navy Austin twelve car from 12–1 in the Green Lion garage, dated that day.

" It smells of scent—*cheap* scent," Norah added emphatically. She became suddenly very wide awake. " We must follow up both trails—either may be the genuine one. Pat, you take Biddie and see what you can find out about the man with the sack. Pixie and Mary, come with me, and we'll sleuth the lady missionary. In exactly one hour from now we'll meet here, but if either party wants help, signal with whistles. Got that?"

.   .   .   .

It proved an elaborate and exciting trail in both directions. Very soon the two little ones realized it was simply an extra well-planned game, and while Pixie was inclined to whine at this Mary's eyes shone behind her spectacles. As she panted down the drive, taking two steps to Norah's one, she asked jerkily:

" Couldn't we do something *back*, Norah—something, you know—that'd be a jolly have for Lady Royston? Couldn't we *really* steal her silver presently and put it all in a sack and take it along and put it down in front of her and say: ' We caught the thief all right. Guides are much better than policemen '?"

" Mary, oh, you gorgeous idiot!" For a moment Norah considered the suggestion. Then she shook her head: " I don't think we'd better. It might be cheek, when we've only seen her once before—and it'd mean going into places in the house without being invited or having permission, which she might feel was bad manners. But don't you worry. We *will* pay her out some way or other later on. The best way to do it now is to find every single clue in this trail much more quickly than she expects us to. Look, those twigs over there are lying in a funny way, is that an arrow by any chance?"

It proved to be one of the arrows " with a box on the end ", as Pixie would call the tracking sign which denotes a hidden letter. Under a mushroom, the indicated seven paces away, they discovered a note which said simply: " The owner of the Navy car ZOG 535 is a member of the A.A."

" Now what's that mean?" Pixie asked, with puckered forehead. " D'you think it's code, Norah?"

" Not it. Come on, kids, there's an A.A. Patrol at White's corner. Their scouts keep a record of every Association car that passes. He'll be able to tell us which way it went—or give us the news Lady Royston's primed him with!"

Grinning, the big, bronzed man in khaki uniform, told them car ZOG 535 had engine trouble when it passed his box, and the young lady driving it had asked the way to the Portland Road by the short cut. Norah only waited to thank him, and all three were soon racing along the grass-grown cart-track which motors occasionally used to save a five-mile detour. Suddenly Pixie, a little ahead of the others, stopped and picked up a clean wash-leather glove, that lay beside a hawthorn bush.

" Do you think——?" she questioned.

Norah took it, looked at it, smelt it, and nodded.

" Same scent," she said curtly. " Hunt around and we'll probably find a track leading into the wood."

This proved correct, and after half an hour of breathless hunting, doubling, false trails and unexpected signs, they came to a place where a drift of leaves lay in a little hollow, and had obviously recently been disturbed. A quick scramble brought to light a large, square biscuit tin. On the lid was chalked the " I have gone home " sign. When they lifted it, it felt heavy.

" I suppose the 'silver' is inside," Norah chuckled, opening the lid.

On top of the untouched layer of attractive fancy biscuits wrapped in silver tinfoil, was a card:

" A reward for good detectives."

" Oh, I say, *isn't* she a sport, Lady Royston, I mean?" Norah said slowly. She had gone rather pink. " Fancy taking so much trouble—I mean—oh, well, I just *do* think some people are marvellous, that's all!"

. . . .

Back at the house they found a grinning Pat and Biddie, who displayed a similar tin, full of old bones with a message which said:

" The poor man with the sack was quite honest—this is where his dog buried his bones. You must look elsewhere for the silver!"

" And it was the most *elaborate* trail, too," Pat

reported, " every single clue—onion, soot and all came in to it. We'd have been completely had, but for Norah!"

Lady Royston nodded.

" I flattered myself the chances were ninety-nine out of a hundred you'd miss the real clue. At this rate, Marigolds, you ought to make bad *or* good, whichever you like, pretty easily. Either takes brains, you know!"

" Will you lay another trail for us—please—*please* —next Saturday?" Pixie begged.

" Well——" Lady Royston hesitated. " As a matter of fact, I've got something to tell you about next Saturday—I shan't be alone here when you come next week. I have just heard that my grandchild, Andrea—the little girl who is a musical genius, and half Hungarian (I told you about her, I believe), is to be sent to me for a holiday. She needs a thorough rest, my daughter tells me, after a long tour of concerts she has just given in France and Germany. Andrea is very highly strung—and although I shall be pleased to have somebody for her to play with once a week, I'm *afraid* I shall have to ask you not to be too strenuous in your games." The old lady's keen eyes softened, and she added, in a lower tone: " My little Andrea is very fragile—a strange child. It will be good for her to make friends with some English Guides."

CHAPTER XI

Mr. Hewlett gives Advice

"Yer see——" Mr. Hewlett took his pipe out of his mouth and knocked the ash from it against his workshop bench. "Yer see, Miss Norah, it's with 'ouses much as it is with 'ats—large or small, plain or fancy, what matters is getting 'em to fit the occasion."

"Yes," Norah agreed gravely. "I do see."

It was early on the Saturday morning following their tracking of Lady Royston's "thief", and they had called by appointment at Mr. Hewlett's house to discuss plans for Ellie's new home. The cross-grained little old foreman had shown himself very friendly since the evening of Norah's accident. He had called twice, on the way from work, to inquire after her arm, and had promised, on hearing the full story of the Marigolds' ambition, to draw out some rough plans and estimates. It was to discuss these that the leader and second had called on him now. They sat on wooden chairs in the little hut behind his house in Foxglove Row, and looked interestedly at the tools on the wall, and the big squares of clean, new wood, leaning against the wall, while Mr. Hewlett talked.

"Some places," Mr. Hewlett continued, "you

want to build for lasting and some again, you don't. Now, if it was for lastingness, brick's the thing—but brick costs money. Yer see, 'tisn't so much a thing itself, it's labour what you pays for, in the building trade, work and workmen's time. Carting bricks, now, to an outlandish sort of spot—three or four lorry loads you'd want—and then a bricklayer's a well-paid man——"

" Well, if not bricks, what are we to build with?" Norah asked. She could see he had an idea.

" I was wondering," he took a catalogue off the bench and turned the pages with a well-licked thumb, " what about a frame 'ut, you know, one of the ready-to-erect sort; what they uses in the army, with a cor-rugated iron roofing and special fire-proof stove hole?"

" Ooh!" Norah and Pat considered the illustration to which he pointed, with critical interest.

" Stands to reason," Mr. Hewlett continued, " I wouldn't recommend such a thing if it wasn't for considerations. But it's a good proverb, ' cut your coat according to your cloth '. That old gipsy party isn't likely to want a house longer than twenty years, and in my experience I've seen the likes of these huts last that, and longer. There's Humbie Camp, now, down by Westbarns—that's been there since the war—streets of frame houses, a big 'all, and a church—I 'elped with putting it together and it was for all the world like a child's box of toys come to full-life size. Fronts and backs, sides and roofs, we unloaded 'em off the lorries, all marked up with A's and B's, ready to fit into each other—couldn't 'ave made mistakes, not if you'd never 'andled a tool in your life until that day——"

" That sounds marvellous," Norah said enthusiastically. " I say, Mr. Hewlett, perhaps if we got a hut like that for Ellie we could put it together ourselves?"

" No knowing what you young ladies could do if you tried!" he chuckled. Then he grew serious. " You could do a tidy part of the work yourselves, Miss, that I tell you straight—or I daresay one or two of the chaps who work with me'd give a hand, in the evenings, with the heavy part of the job, just for the lark of the thing—that young Jimmie Willox now—he is a Scout —spends his Saturdays running around in short trousers, with a pack of little nippers 'e calls ' cubs ', we'll make him do a day's good deed, when the time comes and no mistake!"

Pat interrupted his appreciation of this good joke, by saying anxiously:

" Mr. Hewlett, you haven't told us yet how much money a hut like that is going to cost?"

" Ah, that's the question—I know it is." He became serious again at once, and consulted the index at the back of the catalogue with a stubby first finger. " With a raised floor and double-lined walls, first quality material throughout, a 'ut like that, measuring fifteen foot by eighteen, is—let me see—twenty-and three-five, and two—that's forty-five pounds, five shillings, Miss Norah."

" Forty-five pounds!" Pat's voice was awe-struck.

Norah's chin went up.

"And the cost of getting it down to the place in the woods where Ellie wants to live—I suppose that would be another pound or more even?" she asked.

Mr. Hewlett shook his head.

"No. I see this 'ere firm delivers carriage free to the nearest railway station. I've an old Ford truck in the yard that I let out on hire now and again—we wouldn't need to worry about cost for getting the 'ut down to the woods—them frame 'ouses is all light stuff, anyway, and if need be we could make two—three journeys of it."

"Oh, Mr. Hewlett, that is topping of you!" Norah exclaimed gratefully. "I do think you're kind to help us and take so much trouble. I'm sure this is the best way, that you've found, now. I do feel at last that there's some practical possibility of getting it really done."

"Norah, how can you?" Pat broke in, suddenly letting her impatience get the better of her. "Forty-five pounds is the most enormous lot of money. You know we can't possibly afford it."

"Well, Miss Patsy, you can't build 'ouses for nothing—not by just waving a wand, like it appears they did in the fairy stories," Mr. Hewlett told her briskly. Norah could see he was a little bit annoyed by Pat's trick of harping on the difficulties of the task before them.

But Pat was really worried. Her expression showed it, as she said in a voice that sounded almost sullen:

"Well, you *know* Guides mustn't beg for money, not ever, and unless we ask all the grown-up people we know to subscribe for Ellie's hut I don't see how you even imagine we can get forty-five pounds by September, Norah, and you know Lady Royston said Ellie must have her new house by then——"

"I know—but there are five whole months before September and a few odd days over as well. After all, if you think of it, that only means we've got to make nine pounds a month between us and there are six of us. If you don't count Mary, that's one pound sixteen shillings each, every month—nine shillings a week. Oof—" she blew out her cheeks comically. "Take a bit of doing, won't it, when it's a case of keeping it up regularly? We shall all need a rest cure in the autumn term."

Mr. Hewlett nodded.

"Five shillin's is five shillin's these days," he commented, as though in his experience it had once made quite a different sum, "but I'd say pluck and determination'll see you through with this project, if so be you sticks to it. How about putting in some spare time doing a bit of carpentry for profit, now? Any Tuesday evening I'll be pleased to put you up to making odds and ends, if you care to come round here about six o'clock. You can pay me for the wood you use, and I'll loan you tools to work with—I've a chest full in the corner there as'll be all you need to begin on. But don't you go touching the others you find around here—not on any account. Beginners don't belong to be using my best tools and turning up the edges for me—you understand that, Miss Norah," he added, trying, by this sudden fierceness to do away with any impression that he was such a thing as " soft " in his dealings.

As, half an hour later, they walked away from his green-painted iron gate, up the street of smugly neat Victorian houses, Norah said gratefully:

" I shouldn't wonder if one of the luckiest days our patrol ever had was when we first met that little man. He's completely odd—but that's only the outside parcel he's wrapped in, thank goodness—it was worth hurting my arm ten times over to make friends with him."

Pat looked at her sharply.

" Is it really better again, Norah, really and truly?" she asked.

" Really and truly," Norah nodded.

Pat sighed.

" I'm so glad. It would have been awful to have you really ill, you know. Somehow I do feel we depend on you such a lot, now we're on our own. The kids'd never bother to work or—or anything without you."

" Oh, what complete nonsense. Of course they would—or anyway, if they wouldn't they'd deserve to be scragged. As a matter of fact, Pat, I've often felt it was you who ought to be patrol leader, not me, old thing." Norah slipped her hand confidentially under Pat's arm, as she spoke. " You're so much more sensible and miles a better Guide than I am. You hardly ever forget things, or fly into tempers, or lose your head and go completely fey, the way I do when we get into the woods on a lovely day, and all I want to do is to run and laugh; and play real Brownie games, instead of improving my mind learning what our dear friend Prudence Norton would probably call ' nature study '."

" Well, that's just because I'm made differently," Pat explained. " But it doesn't mean I could lead a patrol. They'd be so bored they'd go to sleep and never wake up. I don't ever have brain-waves as you do—and I shouldn't *dare* to take risks like you do, either."

" Risks?" Norah turned a perfectly innocent face on her solemn second. " You don't imagine *I* take risks, do you?"

Pat's eyelids drooped until she was looking out from under them and her mouth tilted uncontrollably upwards at the corners.

" No," she said gravely. " No. I don't *imagine* it. As a matter of fact, you very seldom give me time!"

CHAPTER XII

Andrea Comes Home

" Oh dear, I do wish Lady Royston's wretched grandchild needn't have come to Stone House just now," Pixie wailed, as once again the patrol climbed the hill towards the upper gate. March was going out with a burst of warm weather—the trees and flowers and birds were all responding to it joyously, but the younger Marigolds wilted in the unaccustomed heat of the Saturday afternoon, as they toiled through the dust of the long road.

" I expect she'll be awfully spoilt," Biddie predicted pessimistically. " She'll have an artistic temperament, and we shall have to give in to her all the time, however much of a little beast she is, because of it being her grandmother's house and estate."

" Well, we needn't ever come here, if she's horrid. Need we, Norah?" Mary questioned, plodding along in her heavy, nailed shoes. "' I mean—there are lots of places else we could go to on Saturdays."

" You kids are always meeting your troubles half way!" Norah complained. " Andrea may be awfully nice, for all we know—anyhow, we've got to put up with her—' a Guide is a friend to all ', remember."

" I expect she'll wear long, velvet frocks with lace collars and cuffs," Pixie predicted.

" Well, if she does, she'll be feeling very hot to-day, poor soul, that's all I can say about it!" Patsy puffed. ' Oh, look, you folks—here's somebody been chalking signs on our gate."

" And for our benefit, too—look at the little orange daisy affair drawn under the arrow—I bet this is another of Lady Royston's surprises, bless her," Norah said affectionately.

" Ooh!" Pixie cheered up. " I didn't think there'd be any more surprises once Andrea was here. It says there's a letter hidden—do let's find it quickly."

Biddie had already scrambled up over the gate, and was on her knees in the bracken, searching.

" Here we are. Shall I read it? It's addressed to The Marigold Patrol all right," she announced, producing an envelope from under the fern.

" Fire away," Norah agreed.

Biddie's expression changed as she opened the letter—she stared at it.

" Horrors!" she remarked briefly.

" What?" Norah asked.

" It's all in French—at least, I think so. It begins ' Chères Amies ', anyway. That's French, isn't it?"

" Let's see it. Give it here," her sister ordered.

The leader and second put their heads together over the page and slowly spelt out the words.

" ' DEAR FRIENDS,

' I am a French Guide. Bandits have made me

a prisoner. I cannot leave the '—*chêne*—what's that?"

" Chain gang?" Pixie suggested brightly.

" Dog, isn't it?" Biddie was more doubtful.

" Oak tree," Mary supplied quietly.

Norah looked at her.

" Sure?" she questioned.

" Yes," Mary nodded.

" ' I cannot leave the oak tree near the little river '."
Norah went on fluently. " Here, I can't get this next
bit at all. Mary, for goodness' sake, if you know any
of the wretched language, come and help. What's
this all about?"

Mary took the paper and squinted at it earnestly;
then her face cleared.

" Oh, easy: ' The Bandit Captain bears a charmed
life. Only by reading the number written on his chest
can you take him captive. But each one of you must be
equally distinguished. In the hollow tree ten paces
south-west of the gate, you will find numbers. Attach
these to the front of your costumes, then come to my
rescue. If the Bandit cries out your number, you are
dead, so take guard to yourselves '."

" Stalking game—what fun," Norah said with
satisfaction. " Andrea can't have come yet after all.
I say, Marigolds, we'll have to be slippy to catch Lady
Royston out. Does anybody know where there is a
big oak tree by the stream?"

" Yes, much farther along than Ellie's cottage,
near where the wood of silver birches starts," Biddie
was quite certain now. " I saw it the first evening,

when we all walked down to Ellie's, do you remember?"

" Here are the numbers." Pat had been hunting around in the meanwhile. " Goodness, if the Bandit's is equally big we ought not to have much difficulty in spotting him!"

She displayed five large postcards, with four figures each three inches high drawn in Indian ink.

" We'll have to be jolly careful if we don't mean to get our own numbers seen," Norah warned them.

" Oh, dear, I'll be no good at all at this. I can't ever see anything in the distance," Mary wailed.

" I can—miles away," Pixie boasted.

" Never mind, Mary," Norah encouraged her recruit. " If it hadn't been for you, we shouldn't know what the game was about. I'll have to polish up my French if this sort of thing is going to happen. It's lucky for us all you could fog it out."

Mary flushed and beamed shyly.

" I thought p'raps I could try and get Interpreter Badge once I'm enrolled," she confided. " D'you think I'd pass?"

" You ought to—you can certainly interpret," Norah assured her thoughtfully. She added, as she fastened one of the cards to the lapel of her blazer: " Come to think of it, I suppose every patrol ought to have at least one interpreter in it, as Guiding's an International Movement.

. . . .

" Three, six, five, one—got you at last !"

Norah, lying flat along the sturdy branch of a

beech tree, spoke exultantly as the slender girl in grey, worming her way through the tall bracken below, turned at a sound in the wood, and for a second left the card on the front of her dress exposed.

She started at the voice, coming from overhead, looked up, and laughed softly. She had thick, dark brown hair, straight to the level of her ears and then curling into a long bob, that suited the alert poise of her small head. Her cheekbones were broad and her chin very pointed, which, together with the queer little peeks to her eyebrows, gave her a puckish, elfin look Norah found attractive.

For a moment they said nothing. Then Norah asked:

"You're Andrea, aren't you?"

The stranger nodded.

"Yes, and you're the patrol leader girl. Grannie betted me I'd never win over you, even if I beat the others. Well, she was right. I didn't think of looking up in the trees for any of you."

Norah chuckled.

"I don't suppose I should have thought of it either, if Chief Scout hadn't told us to ' hide above eye level '," she confessed. "But anyway you've pretty well slaughtered my patrol, haven't you? I should say the honours are even in this game. What have you done with them all?"

"They're talking to Grannie down by the stream, I think. She said to send anybody there I did manage to catch, to help her boil the tea kettle. The little

ones were easy, but the other big girl nearly caught
me twice. It was a nice game, don't you think?"

"It was topping." Norah swung herself into a
sitting position, and dangled her legs. "I say, it's
fun you like games. Are you a Guide yourself?"

"No." Andrea shook her head. She was measuring
the tree with thoughtful eyes. Presently, still talking,
she began to climb up. "No. You see, it's been
difficult, because of moving about so much. Daddie's
in the diplomatic service and he gets shifted from
place to place—and then I tour. But I'd like to be
one." She climbed out on to the branch, and stood,
balancing, her hands on her hips. "Can you do this?"

"Never tried." Norah got rather gingerly to her
feet, then sat down again quickly. "No, it's too thin
a branch. I say, I wish you'd sit down or else hold on
to something."

Andrea laughed. Her teeth were very white, Norah
noticed, and she laughed as if things really amused
her, not in the least self-consciously.

"I can climb anywhere. Watch me." With the
agility of a squirrel she sprang to a higher branch,
caught it with both hands, pulled herself up until
she could get a leg over it, and proceeded to swarm
higher and higher, until Norah called anxiously that
the branches would no longer stand her weight. She
then came down again, hand over hand, and finally
dropped to the ground, laughing and coughing.

"Come on, Grannie'll think we're lost. I expect
tea's ready by now," she panted breathlessly.

Norah, letting herself down more slowly, looked the other girl over with some concern. She was still breathing unevenly, and her colour came and went in quick flushes.

"Aren't you a bit silly to do things like that?" she asked bluntly. Somehow she felt Andrea was a person one could afford to be frank with. "Lady Royston said you'd come here for a rest. That climb's winded you pretty badly."

"Oh, I'm so sick of resting!" Andrea's mouth drooped, and she looked suddenly a lot younger. "I do want to do just as I like, now I've got a holiday. I haven't been home—to this place—for five whole years. You can't think how I've longed to come."

"But you must have ever such exciting times," Norah said curiously. "I mean, playing at concerts and travelling about so much. Don't you like it?"

"No—yes—oh, I don't know." Andrea shrugged. "I suppose I'd hate not to have it all, but just now I'd rather be ordinary and go to school and be a Guide and do the things all other girls do. Please tell me about what you do—you and your patrol."

"Well, we don't seem to do an awful lot, but you'll see if you play with us sometimes." Norah was momentarily at a loss.

"May I? Will you have me?" Andrea asked eagerly.

Norah laughed in her turn. They had come out of the thick part of the wood, and fifty yards away, in a little glade, Lady Royston and the other Marigolds were busy about a fire. At sight of their leader the

Guides abandoned everything else and hurled themselves towards her.

" Who won? Who won?" they inquired breathlessly.

" I did, but only by a ruse that was very nearly cheating," Norah told them. " Andrea's just asking me if she can come out with us again, other days."

" Oh, rather!"

" Yes."

" You bet she can."

" I should jolly well think she could."

There was no mistaking the unanimous shout of enthusiasm. Lady Royston, apparently busy over the kettle, smiled to herself. She was far too observant a Guide to have missed the little chill her announcement of Andrea's return had caused the week before.

" Come and have your teas now," she suggested mildly. " You've spent the whole afternoon on this game, or else I had something to show you."

" Oh, what was it?" Norah asked.

But Lady Royston shook her head.

" One thing at a time. We'll go and see it after tea," she promised mysteriously. " In the meanwhile, and before I forget it, have you any plans for this day fortnight?"

Norah looked thoughtful.

" Is it the third Saturday in the month?" she asked. " Because if so, Patsy and I have to go to the Patrol Leaders' and Seconds' Divisional Meeting, I'm afraid. Captain wrote to me and said we could still go, although the company is suspended, and somehow I think she wanted us to."

" I see, well, it doesn't matter," Lady Royston said: " We shall have plenty of time for the expedition I had in mind later on. What are the others doing, while you're at the meeting?"

Before anyone could reply, Andrea said with decision:

" They're coming to play with me, Grannie—all day—lunch and everything, please."

The three younger Marigolds, looking into her dancing eyes, felt suddenly that the prospect was one of the most exciting things in life. Norah, remembering the episode of the tree climbing, wondered a little anxiously just what games Andrea would choose for her patrol. Certainly, since they wished to avoid a dull life, she suspected Andrea was going to be a distinct asset to the pirate crew.

CHAPTER XIII

Andrea Takes Command

" You don't want to garden any more—not now surely? We gardened all the morning and all yesterday evening, and all of every evening for weeks and weeks and weeks," Andrea exaggerated, flinging herself into a deck chair on the verandah at Stone House, after lunch on the Saturday of the patrol leader's conference.

Biddie, Pixie and Mary, clustered in the doorway, looked at one another.

" Norah does want us to get on with the herb garden and it's rather fun, the way it's beginning to look like a real garden, not just a wild patch of weeds," Biddie ventured.

" Oof! Those weeds! It makes my back ache to think of them," Andrea groaned. " Now, be sports, let's go out somewhere and do something exciting. I'm so dreadfully bored with gardening. It's different for you. You all go to school, and see people and have friends. I'm all by myself all day, with Grannie and the servants here, and although I do love it for a bit, it would be nice to do something quite different for a change. I know! Let's go over to Chagleigh on a bus, and go to the pictures. There's ever such a thrilling cowboy film; Betty, the kitchen maid, told me all about it. I've got five shillings. I'll invite you all."

"How lovely. I'd adore to do that." Pixie, who had a great weakness for the pictures and was seldom allowed to go, danced up and down in excitement.

Mary, to whom such an outing was also, though for different reasons, a very rare treat, said solemnly: "It's awf'lly nice of you, Andrea."

Biddie hesitated. She wished Norah and Patsy were there to sanction the outing, for, although no actual promise had been given, she knew her leader and second were taking it for granted the afternoon would be spent on the patrol's latest good turn.

This—Lady Royston's secret of a fortnight before— was no less a job than the restoration of the old, sunken herb plot, beyond the lily pools and the kitchen garden. It had been neglected for years, and Lady Royston admitted that, but for Ellie and her Gipsy lore, it might well have gone on being neglected for a great many more.

"I never let the gardeners touch it, because the average gardener doesn't know the difference between herbs and weeds, in a great many cases," she had confided. "My husband's mother was the last person who took an active interest in such things, I believe. (We've got a book of recipes she wrote that might amuse you, some day.) She didn't make the plot, though. It dates from Tudor times, I believe. In any case, properly put in order, and re-stocked, it might be a curiosity, and your old gipsy friend is welcome to gather simples in it whenever she likes, provided she'll give you advice as to what things are and where they belong."

Pleased to find a job so ready on their hands, the Marigolds had lost no time in getting to work. Biddie thought with satisfaction of the clipped grass on the four steep banks that surrounded the square, and the paths of brick, bordered with very long-legged and undisciplined box-edging, which were coming to light. Ellie had entered into the plan, and given a fund of advice, in which were mingled long dissertations on the uses of thyme and sage, rosemary, chirvil, rue and parsley, as well as all the rarer herbs and some of the more flourishing weeds which they discovered. Biddie sighed a little, remembering how very firmly Lady Royston had discouraged her from trying out some of the gipsy remedies.

" You leave doctoring to qualified people like your father, my dear," Lady Royston had said with emphasis. " First Aid is very useful, but let it be the sort that is thoroughly reliable. I'm far from denying Ellie's wood wisdom, and I dare say a great many of her concoctions work excellently—but dirt's dirt and germs are germs, and _I_ wouldn't like to use any poultice, plaster, pill or potion she'd brewed in that dreadful little shack of hers—and I'm sure all your parents would agree with me."

" Look here, are we going, or aren't we?" Andrea's voice, a trifle impatient, broke through Biddie's reflections. Just occasionally the elder girl's experience as a flattered and brilliant young musician gave her a certain air of command much older than her age, and very difficult to withstand. Biddie, reassured by a sense that Andrea was, after all, very nearly a grown-up, and quite as much to be followed as Norah, accordingly, said slowly:

" I think it would be fun, yes, I'd like to do that. We'll be back by six o'clock, to meet Norah and Pat, won't we?"

" Rather! Why, we'll probably be back by tea time if we start now," Andrea assured her easily. " Grannie won't mind. She's busy in the orchid house to-day—somebody's sent her some new ones or something. She probably won't even notice we've gone."

" Oughtn't you—we—to ask permission to go?" Mary inquired a little anxiously.

Andrea tossed her head.

" Goodness, no, child. I'm not a baby any more. Why, when I'm at home, I do exactly as I like all day long provided I get in my practising."

As they walked down the drive together, Pixie asked curiously:

" Do you have to practise an awful, *awful* lot, Andrea?"

" Oh, about six or eight hours a day," Andrea said indifferently. " I love it. I expect it's because I wasn't supposed to touch my fiddle for a fortnight that I've got a sort of restless feeling. I miss it all the time. But I'd been doing too much, my wrist needed resting."

" I'm glad you'll be allowed to play soon," Mary said seriously. " I do love music. Mummie's got a record of you playing a Mozart dance, on the gramophone, and I always liked it."

" What—the Minuet in G?" Andrea flushed with pleasure. " Oh, I made that record more than a year ago. I play better now."

Once outside the shade of the trees they realized it was a very hot afternoon. There was a dusty, brassy light over everything, and not a breeze stirred anywhere.

Biddie, glancing at the sky, said anxiously:

" I do hope it isn't going to be a thunderstorm. We ought to have brought macks."

" Nonsense!" Andrea laughed. " Why, I'm glad I even left my cardigan at home. It's almost as hot as in Hungary. Only there we go to sleep all the afternoon and don't feel it."

" I thought Hungary was ever so cold, with sledges and snow and things?" Pixie queried.

" So it is in the winter, stupid, only it's as hot in summer as it is cold at Christmas, see?" Andrea explained impatiently.

By the village church they learned from people waiting for the afternoon bus that they would have to change at Brenton, the next little town, to get to Chagleigh, as they had missed the direct bus.

" All the more fun," Andrea said happily. " I like towns."

Brenton, however, is not a very exciting place. It

is rather dirty and small and busy, strung along a narrow main street, with cheap shops on either side and a big public house in the middle, where all the buses stop. Andrea turned up her nose at it, and was inclined to be cross when the Chagleigh bus proved late in arriving. Crowds of people with shopping baskets were waiting on the pavement, and presently a poor old man appeared in the gutter, with a fiddle and began scraping out a thin tune, in the hope of pennies.

Andrea put her hands over her ears and grimaced.

" Tell me when he stops," she begged.

Mary, looking at him closely, plucked at her arm.

" Don't be unkind, Andrea," she begged wistfully, " he looks dreadfully down and out and he can't play better than that—his hands are all stiff with rheumatism. Don't show him you hate his music."

" Well, I *do* hate it," Andrea grumbled, but she condescended not to show the fact quite so obviously and presently took a good look at the old musician. Her face softened. " Heavens, kids, how awful to come to that, if you'd ever been able to really play well. Oh, *no*—I just can't bear the Prize Song—wait —stop!"

Before the other three realized what she was up to she had darted across the pavement, slipped a coin into the battered hat on the kerb, and was talking animatedly to the shabby, bent figure. The old man looked bewildered, but presently handed over his violin and bow, reluctantly, into Andrea's hands.

"I say—she's going to play—but how awful of her!" Pixie exclaimed, half scandalized, half thrilled.

"She mustn't—it'll make a scene," Biddie said unhappily.

Mary, her eyes very bright, said slowly:

"She does play beautifully—listen—isn't it lovely?"

High over the rattle and hum of the rickety little town there rose suddenly the clear, throbbing lilt of a violin touched by a skilful hand. The notes rang true and pure, swinging into the silver triumph of Wagner's "Master Singers".

Up and down the street people paused, turned and stared at the nicely dressed girl, standing in the gutter, her cheek laid to the greasy wood of the old beggar's violin, her long arm making the bow fly over the frayed gut of the strings. The man himself stared at her as though he very much doubted his own senses. It seemed to the Marigolds that she was glad simply to have a violin under her hands again—she had forgotten everything else. She was smiling a little, swaying in rhythm to the music, turning and twisting it in mid career, making it do odd, exciting things, switching it through clever modulations from one well-known tune to another. Ten minutes had passed, and the crowd on the pavement was dense, when she brought the performance suddenly to a close, tossed the old man his fiddle, and picking up his hat, went round collecting quite a harvest of pennies from the onlookers, who stared and whispered behind her back.

" Now, Grandfather, you can take a holiday for the rest of the day," she told him kindly.

Suddenly she seemed to realize the curious glances following her. She flushed, tossed her head, and beckoning the Marigolds, hurriedly climbed on to a bus that had just drawn up, and made her way quickly to the front seat, Pixie and Mary instinctively following her.

" But, Andrea, this isn't our bus—this is going to Fransham Common," Biddie protested.

Apparently no one heard her, and by the time she, too, had reached the front seat, the bus was already jolting down the street and out of the town.

Andrea had flopped on to the seat, her legs sprawled out in front of her, and was fanning herself vigorously with a big white silk handkerchief.

" Oh, glory, that's the sort of thing I do!" she complained. " Biddie, I couldn't help it, really I couldn't, he looked so old and depressed and poor, I just *had* to make something exciting happen for him. Did you *see* how thrilled he was? Oh, but I suppose I did look a fool, didn't I? Was it a dreadfully stupid thing to do?"

" I think it was marvellous of you," Pixie burst out excitedly. " Ever so romantic and adventury, and ever such a good turn. There must have been lots of money—more than five shillings—in that hat, and the poor old man wouldn't have made more than one, the dreadful whiny tune he was playing. It was ever such a real good turn," she repeated.

" Andrea, you play gorgeously, I think," Mary put in eagerly. " Doesn't she, Biddie?"

Despairingly, Biddie dropped into the nearest seat.

" *This is the wrong bus*, I tell you!" she repeated. " It's not going to Chagleigh at all."

" Oh, *that* doesn't matter," Andrea said calmly. " Why should we go to Chagleigh? I can't even remember why we thought we'd go there. Let's go somewhere else!"

CHAPTER XIV

Marigolds at the Fair

" I think a fair's lots more fun than the pictures. It was absolute Providence that put us on that wrong bus," Biddie admitted, a good two hours later, as, with a coconut under her arm, and a cupid doll mascot pinned on her school tie, she strolled along between the booths at Fransham Common.

" I've never won anything in my life before." Mary hugged a large and loud-voiced alarm clock with a picture of Mickey Mouse on the glass, jealously close. " Mummie will be so pleased when I tell her. We'll be able to put it in the kitchen when we have a home again."

" You had enough shots before you got it!" Andrea teased her.

" Oh, well, I don't care, I *meant* to win it," Mary told her, and added with a sigh, " I *am* a rotten shot, I own."

" I wish I'd won something," Pixie mourned.

" Never mind. Let's go up in the swing-boats, and then have ices," Andrea suggested. " May as well try all the fun, now we are here."

She had been in a mad frame of mind ever since

the episode of the beggar violinist, and the sight of the striped tents, merry-go-rounds, and caravans on Fransham Common had given the final tip to her irresponsibility. She had at once suggested visiting the fair, and the others had agreed with enthusiasm.

" You say you like adventures—I bet we'll get some there," she had predicted.

So far, beyond a ride on a so-called ghost train, the biggest thrill had been Mary's unexpected success at the pop-gun shooting range. Pixie insisted on heading back there, ice cream cornet in hand, a little later.

" I do so very much want to win something like Mary has," she wailed, the spoilt-child whine, which Norah and Patsy so firmly discouraged, well in evidence.

The little booth had a shelf in front of it, where the burly owner — a rough-looking customer in a red flannel shirt—laid out prizes in a tempting array.

" Ooh, look what he's put in place of the clock! Aren't they lovely?" Pixie clasped her hands ecstatically before the small wire cage, containing two live love birds.

" Poor little things. They're awfully frightened," Biddie said pityingly.

Andrea frowned.

" What a shame to cramp them up in that tiny cage. Look, they simply knock themselves to pieces when they flutter. Oh, I think it's cruel!"

" Easy remedy, lady. You hit the bull's-eye that has their number on, and they belong to you. Lovely little pets they make—live for years!" The man in the red shirt leered at Andrea invitingly. " Threepence a go—four shots a shilling. Cost you a fortune, those birds would, in a fancier's shop. Turquoise Budrigas they are. Try your luck, Miss, and win 'em for three-pence."

" Come on—let's try," Biddie urged Andrea.

Andrea, however, needed no urging. She had already paid out her shilling, and was carefully testing the toy gun the man handed her. The Marigolds, impressed by her manner, waited hopefully. To their disappointment and her annoyance, all three shots went wide of the target.

" Here, you try," she handed the gun to Biddie and felt for another shilling. " Oh, bother, I haven't got any more money."

" I've got sixpence—and a shilling," Biddie handed over the two coins without a thought.

Her first shot landed wide, the second was on the circle next the bull's-eye, and a squeal of excitement proved just how seriously the younger Marigolds were following the game. Two more were wasted. The fifth and sixth, exasperatingly, went to join the second.

" Let me try. Oh, please do let me try now!" Pixie begged. The man in charge smiled at her in an almost fatherly fashion, as she paid for three shots, and took her stand deliberately. She was almost sobbing, when her luck proved no better than the others.

" Mary, you try. You won before," she reminded the Marigold's recruit.

" Yes, but——" Mary hesitated.

" Oh, go on, be a sport," Biddie urged. " We just *must* get those poor little birds. 'A Guide is kind to animals ', you know."

Mary sighed. She had gone rather pale, and Biddie had a fleeting wonder if ice cream did not agree with her. However, she counted out three pennies and said politely to the stall-keeper:

" Please may I have a different gun? Not this one. The green one I had last time."

The man seemed a little startled, then laughed it off.

" Bless me, if she doesn't want the one I always use myself! Did you have that before, my dear? Well, here it is, and good luck to you."

Mary took the gun, heaved another deep sigh, then to the horror of the others, raised it, shut her eyes tight and fired.

The stall-keeper's not altogether pleased exclamation roused them.

" Well, jigger my buttons—clean in the bull's eye it is, and very first shot off!"

.   .   .   .

" Andrea, d'you mean you really haven't got any more money? You're ragging, aren't you?" Biddie spoke anxiously, a few minutes later.

The four of them had walked away from the shooting range, bearing the love birds triumphantly along with them. Once beyond the fringe of the crowd gathered round it, they had stopped for a council of war.

Andrea shook her head.

"I've spent every penny," she admitted, quite unashamed.

"So have I," Biddie groaned.

"And me," Pixie nodded ungrammatically, adding tragically, "I *did* so want the little love birds, Biddie."

"You can have them, Pixie," Mary said generously. "You see, I'd never be allowed to keep them, where I live, or anyway, I didn't specially want them—only to sort of rescue them."

"Oh, Mary, you darling!" Pixie hugged her in enthusiastic gratitude, then carefully took over the cage, chirruping at the frightened little inmates in an encouraging and proprietary fashion.

"Mary, was it your last threepence you paid?" Biddie asked.

Mary nodded.

"Yes, my church threepence for to-morrow," she owned. "Mrs. Morris'll be awf'lly cross, but I thought what it says in the Litany about 'Have mercy on all prisoners and captives', and I thought maybe I could explain about it all right, even if Mrs. Morris doesn't understand what I explain!"

When they had finished laughing, Biddie said anxiously:

"But look here, this means we'll have to *walk* home, do you realize? We can't go on a bus without any money to pay for tickets—and it's simply miles and miles."

Andrea shivered.

" What a fag! Still, it doesn't matter really—it's
lots cooler now the sun's gone in. How far are we
from Stone House, do you imagine?"

" Almost ten miles, the way we came. But I believe
there is a way over the fields, avoiding Brenton. Let's
ask somebody."

A tall, gipsy - looking lad answered their inquiry
in a friendly fashion, and gave a grinning reply, when
Andrea, at parting, threw him a word or two over her
shoulder in a language the others did not understand.

" What did you say?" Biddie asked curiously.

" Oh, just wished him luck in Romany speech.
Can't you rockrapan Romani, pen comly?" Then,
as they stared, she threw back her head and laughed,
" that means, ' Can't you talk gipsy language, sister
dear,'" she explained. "You see, out on the Hungarian
plains, where we go for holidays, there are lots and
lots of gipsies. I had a gipsy nurse for a time when
I was little, too. I thought I wouldn't tell you just at
first, so I didn't pretend to know about your Ellie.
Anyway, it doesn't matter much. Oh, bother, I do
believe it's going to rain. Look how dark the sky is
over there."

They had come out on the edge of the road that
crossed the Common, beyond the fair ground. In
front of them a foot path, which the gipsy had advised
them to follow, straggled away between gorse and
brambles, to a white stile, leading across fields. Now,
out of the shelter of the booths, they could see storm
clouds, very dark and threatening, coming up from the

west. Andrea shivered again, and hugged herself with both arms.

" I do wish I'd brought a blazer," she complained. " Let's hurry, Biddie. I'm just freezing, aren't you?"

Biddie, glancing at her watch, said nothing. It was past five, a storm was coming, they were at least seven miles from home, and she had only the vaguest idea of the way. Suddenly, and from the bottom of her heart, she wished Norah and Patsy were with them. But Norah and Patsy, by now on their way back from the Leader's Conference, did not even know that they had gone out, and no one—no one at all—had the faintest idea as to what direction they had taken.

CHAPTER XV

The Gipsy Call

"I can't go any farther, Biddie—really I can't. These silly shoes have skinned all my heels. Please let me stay and rest—you go on," Pixie begged.

Biddie snorted.

"Your heels'll feel far worse when you start again, if you stop now. They'll be all stiff and stuck to your stockings. And what *is* the point of sitting in soaking clothes anyway?" she argued. "Oh, Pixie, don't be stupid! That ground's as wet as a bath-sponge. Do get up and come along."

"I can't," Pixie protested, and began to cry.

Biddie looked at her, then at Andrea and Mary. All four were draggled, mud stained, soaked to the skin and tired out. The promised storm had broken ten minutes after they left the fair, with a little thunder and lightning and a very thorough downpour. Now, two hours later, it was still raining, with a steady, drizzling rain that looked like setting in for the night. Ahead and behind them, between tangled hedges, stretched a grass-grown, deserted road. They were completely and most desolately lost.

Andrea, her wet cotton frock sticking to her thin

shoulders, her long hair dripping in rats' tails over her white face, said impatiently:

" Stop being a baby, Pixie, and come on. The road must lead somewhere."

Pixie's sobs grew more aggrieved.

" I'm not a baby. You made us come, it's all your fault," she complained incoherently.

Mary, a ridiculous little figure, with her alarm clock pushed up under her jersey for protection, and her glasses misted with rain, said stoutly:

" If we go on we must come to a house in the end—or maybe a gipsy camp or something. There have been gipsy fires all along the way we've come. Buck up, Pixie. I'll help you. You can lean on me."

Pixie, however, her nerve completely broken, merely wailed afresh.

" I d-don't like gipsies any more. I'm afraid of gipsies. I want to be at home—I do—I do!"

Andrea, between impatience and pity, turned away and began to walk on again. Suddenly she paused, listening, then, throwing back her head, gave a long drawn-out cry.

" *Hup-hup-Rom-ma-ny, Rom-ma-ny joter!*"

She repeated it, in a clear, sing-song shout, two or three times, only stopping when it made her cough. From away to the left, beyond the tall hedge, a faint answering cry drifted back.

Still coughing, her hand on her side, as though she had got a stitch, Andrea turned back to the others.

" Mary's right. There are gipsies," she panted

triumphantly. " A Hungarian gipsy taught me that call and he *said* if I was ever lost, to use it, only I'd forgotten. Listen, *Ro-ma-ny chal akai*!" she repeated the answering call, and added: " Gipsies all over the world call out that way and answer like that when they're lost. He'll think we're gipsies too, what fun!"

Biddie, however, was not so sure it was fun, as a big, rough-looking man swung himself over a stile in the hedge, dropped into the road and then paused, staring at them with a heavy frown. He wore poor clothes, but had a brilliant silk scarf round his throat and a gold watch chain. His black hair was very thick and grew down in side-whiskers that gave him a Spanish look. Pixie, thoroughly scared, scrambled up off the wet ground and even Mary retreated a few steps. Andrea, however, went forward at once and began to talk rapidly, gesticulating in a foreign way. Slowly the man's face cleared. He looked keenly at the damp, depressed trio on the far side of the road, then at Andrea again—nodding meanwhile. Presently Andrea called out joyfully:

" Biddie, we're absolutely miles from the Stone House still. We must have walked in a circle, but it doesn't matter; this gentleman says he'll drive us home. He says we're nearly back to Fransham Common —his camp's on the edge of it!"

.   .   .   .

As they rattled, jolted and banged along the road, in an ancient Ford car, the hood up and the side-curtains flapping like thunder, Biddie murmured to Andrea:

" I think we were awfully lucky. Some horrid person might have come when you called. This gipsy's nice."

Andrea said slowly:

" Only a real gipsy would have answered. The tramping people don't know Romany any more. Real gipsies are always gentlemen——"

Her voice trailed away.

Biddie looked at her anxiously.

" Are you so awfully tired, Andrea?"

" No, but my head aches and I've got a hateful stitch. It hurts me to talk," Andrea admitted.

" Then don't talk," Biddie advised sensibly.

When at last, well after dark, their rescuer stopped at the steps of Stone House, the front door stood wide open, and in the light streaming from the hall they could see anxious figures gathered.

" Oh, we are going to get into a row!" Biddie predicted miserably. She had recognized her father, a tall and active silhouette, behind Lady Royston's ample curves, and the bustling daintiness of Pixie's frantically agitated Mamma.

" We're all right, Grannie, and we've had ever such fun, and lots of adventures." Andrea, getting out of the car first, made a gallant effort to draw the grown-ups' fire. But the lighted steps reeled before her eyes, and she had to clutch at Biddie for support as the unbearable pain, like a red-hot knitting needle, jabbed in her side again.

" Andrea's not well. We were soaked and I think

she's got a chill," Biddie explained, a trifle jerkily, and added, " It was all our fault. I ought to have taken a coat."

" Soaked, I should just think you are!"

" Where have you been?"

" What have you been doing?"

" Why didn't you leave any message?"

The questions rained on them. They became aware that Norah and Patsy, still in uniform, were among the people pressing round them. Then Lady Royston pushed her way unceremoniously to the front.

" Andrea, you're a naughty, tiresome girl, and I shall never be able to trust you again. Go straight to bed," she ordered. Then, as Andrea murmured something: " Of course, I'll pay the man who drove you home. Go up to your room, Miss, I'll come to you there. As to you others—you Marigold Guides—you've made enough trouble this afternoon to last a long while, unless I'm very happily mistaken."

" We're awfully sorry——" Biddie began, but Lady Royston snapped her up.

" If Andrea has pneumonia again, your being sorry won't help in the least. I thought as Guides I could trust you, but I see I can't. You've no sense, and you're completely unreliable. I'm very much disappointed in you all."

" That's not fair——!" Pixie began indignantly, still clutching her cage of exhausted love birds. Her own mother, however, hushed her.

" Be quiet, darling, you've been a silly little girlie,

and Lady Royston's quite right. Do you know it's very nearly nine o'clock? Mummie won't be able to let you go on being a Guide if you do things like this, will she?"

Norah, already smarting under the fact that her patrol had made such fools of themselves, writhed at this baby talk. Rather stiffly, she said to Lady Royston:

" We're all very sorry, Lady Royston, but accidents happen to everybody. I think we ought to hear what made them go out without leaving any message, and why they are so late back, don't you?"

Lady Royston, however, was eaten up with anxiety for Andrea and accordingly in a towering rage.

" Hoyty-toyty, young lady, don't begin telling me what I ought and ought not to do, after what's happened," she admonished impatiently. " Your patrol's stuck to its intention of ' making bad ' with a vengeance to-day."

The tone, more than the words, made the colour come up in Norah's cheeks.

" If you feel that way we won't come here any more—not ever," she said in a low voice.

It is rather doubtful if Lady Royston heard the challenge, however, for just at that moment Dr. Ormonde, who had been questioning Biddie closely, came forward—a tall, grey-haired, kindly man, with a calm manner that banished panic.

" Lady Royston, I'm sure you must be longing to get rid of us all at this hour," he said pleasantly, " and my wife will be getting very anxious. If Mrs. Lloyd will allow me, I can take her and her daughter, as well as the other wanderers, back to Oakleigh. But while I am here, would you, perhaps, like me to take a look at your grand-daughter and make sure she is not going to suffer any ill effects from to-day's ducking? Often, you know, one can take these things in time——"

He left the sentence unfinished, and Biddie squeezed his hand. Punishment would be forthcoming for her part in the day's bad deeds, her knowledge of her father left her no reason to doubt, but her chief worry would be allayed if only she could be sure there was nothing seriously wrong with Andrea.

When, a little later, Dr. Ormonde came downstairs, however, he was alone, and he looked rather serious.

" That girl is in for a sharp attack of pleurisy, I'm afraid," he told Pixie's mother as she fluttered forward, all anxious questions. " However, we've packed her into blankets and if she's no better to-morrow I'll send in a nurse. Now—forward march, all of you—one casualty is quite enough from one outing. I don't want any more patients on my hands. Mustard baths and hot lemons for the Marigold Patrol—and we'll put off explanations until to-morrow morning!"

CHAPTER XVI

A Bad Half-hour

" I think you're the limit—the absolute, hopeless, sickening limit."

Pale and resentful, her eyes blazing, Norah faced a chastened patrol, gathered in the tool shed, preparatory to a visit to Mr. Hewlett for carpentry instruction. It was Tuesday evening, and by ordinary standard her wrath over their Saturday escapade should have been cooling, but Patsy had warned Biddie and Biddie had warned the others that on this occasion Norah was going to be difficult to appease.

" I couldn't tell you what I thought of you on Saturday. You were too tired, for one thing, and anyway, Lady Royston didn't give me much chance to get a word in. But I want to tell you now that there wasn't a single thing she said to all of us that I don't say to you. You know perfectly well I don't expect you to be little goody-goodies, but I do expect you to have some sense, and some gumption, and to remember one or two out of the ten Laws, even if you can't keep them all, yet."

" Oh, Norah, don't be a beast," Biddie begged.

" It was a horrid, hateful day, and we'll never be silly like that again. Honest, we won't."

" Andrea made us—really she did," Pixie complained. " It was all her idea to go and——"

" Shut up, Pixie!" Norah cut her short unceremoniously. " Putting the blame on poor Andrea, who's so ill she may be going to die, isn't specially sporting. Anyway, Andrea's clever and a genius, and she's not a Guide. You ought to have looked after Andrea."

" Why, she's years and years older than we are!" even Biddie flamed into open rebellion, " and she's never tried to make *you* do anything yet. I bet if she did, you'd do it, Norah. She's so jolly strong, sort of——"

" You're all so jolly weak, and no ' sort of ' to it," Norah complained. " It's the silliness of the whole thing that makes me so cross. You just did as she suggested like three sheep following a fourth over a road, *baa-baa*, and no matter what traffic's coming. You hadn't the manners to tell Lady Royston where you were going, or the gumption to take macs with you, in case it rained, or the sense to remember a Guide is thrifty and not spend every penny you'd got between you. Even after all that, if you'd found your own way back I could have forgiven you better, but you must top all by getting lost not ten miles from home, in country that just absolutely, literally bristles with signposts. What *do* you call yourselves?"

Biddie heaved a sigh.

" I suppose we are rather tenderfoots," she admitted.

" Rather? *Rather?*" Norah shook her head. The worst of her exasperation was wearing off, but she was still indignant. " And Patsy and I, at the Divisional P.L.'s meeting, were entering you for the County Patrol Competition while you were giving that exhibition of yourselves."

" What a hope!" Patsy commented inelegantly. It was her first contribution to the discussion. Experience had taught her that when Norah was really roused the best way was to let her talk herself to a standstill.

Mary, looking rather more scared-rabbit than usual, ventured to ask tentatively:

" What is a County Patrol Competition exactly, please?"

Norah sighed.

" A competition open to representative patrols—one from each company in the county," she explained. " As we're the only active patrol left in 6th Oakleigh we can enter for it, and it's a big chance, because otherwise we'd have had to prove we were the best patrol in the company first. All the others are doing that. Nobody knows what exactly the competition will be. It's for ' General Guiding—up to the standard of the Second Class Test ', the Commissioner said."

" And each patrol has to produce one Guide who hasn't got 2nd class yet, and one quite new recruit, so there's evidently going to be a chance for Pixie and Mary to do their bit," Pat reminded her.

Mary's eyes shone.

" How lovely!" she said simply.

Pixie hugged herself.

" Ooh, I hope it'll be something I can do. When is the competition, and where's it going to be, Norah?"

" Three months hence—August," Norah told them. " The place is the one snag, as far as Pat and I can see. It's to be at Barham Towers, near Welworth. It's miles from here, and it's going to cost us nearly seven shillings each for fares, as far as Pat and I can discover."

The Marigolds looked at one another.

" I won't be able to go, then," Mary said decidedly.

" I simply hate asking Daddie for fourteen whole shillings for the two of us," Pat admitted.

" None of us ought to afford it, really, not if we're going to carry out our scheme for Ellie," Norah agreed. " But Pat and I didn't realize how far it was when we put down our names. It was only when we went to the station afterwards and inquired, we realized we'd made a mistake. But I wish we could think of a plan for getting there, because if by any chance we did at all decently, it'll be the end of August, and quite near the beginning of term, and it might help to influence Miss Nesbitt about reopening the company, I thought."

" Couldn't we walk there, camping on the way?" Pat suggested thoughtfully.

" I don't think any of our people'd let us—and anyway, it'd take two or three days, and we'd probably look like tramps when we arrived. There are going to be marks for inspection," Norah reminded her.

" Couldn't we, maybe, ask Lady Royston to lend us her car?" Pixie questioned, blandly.

" No, that we certainly could not!" Norah was emphatic. " Lady Royston's utterly, entirely, absolutely fed up with us, and I don't wonder at it."

She sighed, as she spoke. She had taken a very great personal liking to the fierce and sometimes ungracious, but straight-driving old lady, under whose brusqueness she had sensed so much sterling kindness from the first. She felt Mary's solemn gaze fixed on her, and shrugged away from the subject, glancing at her watch.

" We ought to be at Mr. Hewlett's. Come on. We'll talk more about the competition another time," she said quickly.

To her surprise, Mary demurred, the shy red mounting in her sallow little face.

" Norah—would you mind—might I—I mean, I'm not much good at carpentry anyway. Need I come to-night?"

" No, not if you've anything special to do, of course you needn't, child," Norah told her kindly. There was a funny, suppressed excitement about the Marigolds' youngest recruit that her P.L. had noticed vaguely all the evening.

Mary wriggled.

" Only—you see, I heard from Mummie this morning," she confessed. " She's got a case quite near here, and she said maybe, when she got her two hours off, she'd come and see me. I couldn't bear not to be in when she came!"

" I should jolly well think you couldn't!" Norah agreed. " Run along at once, and good luck to you. I hope ever so much she'll come."

.   .   .   .

" You 'aven't what I call got your minds on the work this evening. What's come to you all? Are you worried about something?"

Old Mr. Hewlett, his head on one side, scrutinizing a very badly set plane he had just rescued from Biddie, suddenly turned on the Marigolds, with one of his unexpected, abrupt outbursts.

They all jumped.

Norah put down the two pieces of wood she had been glueing for a bracket, and said slowly:

" How did you guess?"

Mr. Hewlett shook his head.

" Nothing gives away h'anxiety like any shape or form of 'andywork," he told them. " You got to do 'andywork with your brain *and* your fingers—fingers alone can't make a job of it. Now last week, you was all getting along very promising and careful. But to-day the very way you 'andles your tools tells me there's something laying on your minds. Maybe if you was to tell me about it, now——?"

Norah heaved a sigh.

" We're worried about such a lot of things, aren't we, Pat?" She appealed to her second. " Most of all we're worrying about Andrea, of course, because she's got pleurisy and is ever so ill, and it's our fault, in a way. And then, there's Ellie's house—we aren't getting any nearer to buying that—and now there's the patrol competition."

Somehow, old Mr. Hewlett, in his shirt-sleeves and his inevitable bowler hat, encouraged confidences. Leaving their tools on the bench, the Marigolds gathered round him, explaining their troubles, while he sucked at his short briar pipe and scratched his nose meditatively, and said:

" Ah!" and " That so?" and " I follow, Miss Norah " in a way that made one feel he was giving each problem his full and practical attention. At the end, he said seriously:

" Now, it's a funny thing—a very funny thing—but you saying about this here Rally that's to be held at Barham Towers. I was speaking to Jim Willox about that place, only yesterday, asking him where it is, and that. I've a contract to deliver a load of gravel there by my lorry, for Timmins & Co., once a month. Now, if you young ladies wasn't too partickler, I dessay we could arrange for that load to go over the same day as your Rally business, and you could travel along with it. Jim'd wait and bring you back after. We'd fix you up with a tarpaulin or two, so's you wouldn't mess yourselves up too much—gravel *is* messy stuff."

" Oh, Mr. Hewlett, do you really mean it?" Patsy asked.

" You angel!" Norah exclaimed earnestly.

Mr. Hewlett chuckled.

"Well, it won't cause me any inconvenience—only a bit of contriving—so I don't see as I'm qualified to put me wings on just yet," he disdained their thanks. "Why, what's happened now? Has the end of the world come, or have you won the Irish Sweep, Miss Mary?"

This as, heedless of everything but her own excitement, small Mary scampered down the garden steps outside, into the workshop and flung herself on to Norah.

"Oh, Norah, Norah! What do you think?" she panted.

"I don't," Norah told her resignedly. "What is it, Mary?"

"Mother's come to nurse Andrea! Isn't it gorgeous and splendiferous and thrilling? She'll be here at least three weeks, she says. Lady Royston insists. And Andrea's going to get better. Mummie says she is. I think she's the loveliest person ever, because although she was so ill she remembered about my mother being a nurse and her name and everything, and she kept on and on asking to be allowed to have her. She made them promise to keep it a secret surprise for me, too. Mummie wouldn't stay more than a few minutes to-day, because Andrea's still quite badly ill —she just stopped long enough to tell me—but later on I'll see her lots, and anyway it's heavenly to think of her so near. Oh, and Norah, I nearly forgot, Andrea's made Lady Royston forgive us, and we're all to go to

Stone House on Saturday, same as we usually do, and maybe, if we're good, Mummie says she'll let you and Pat go and see Andrea anyway, and all of us if she's well enough. Isn't it marvellous?"

Norah sat down on a sawing trestle.

"It's much too good to be true—all of it," she said solemnly.

Again Mr. Hewlett chuckled.

"What did I say? Shine and shadder—shadder and shine again—that's life, that is," he announced sententiously. "Young ladies, the time fer your carpentry class is up. I 'ope you'll all pay a deal of attention next week, for between one thing and another we haven't done as much work to-day as'd go on a bee's knee!"

CHAPTER XVII

Andrea has an Idea

" I've been thinking." Andrea, lying back rather limply against the piled up pillows in the big carved wooden bed, stared at the ceiling. " Thinking *and* thinking. It hasn't been dull, being ill, because I'd got such a lot to think about."

Norah, curled up on the bottom of the bed, glanced appreciatively round the long, low room, with its old-fashioned furniture of polished oak, its kindly, faded chintzes, and the bowl of early columbines, dainty as dancing ladies, on the low table in the window.

" This is a lovely place to think *in*," she commented. " But are you really and truly getting better, now, Andy?"

" Yes." Andrea put out one long thin hand and patted the shining curve of the violin that lay on the quilt beside her. " Nurse let me practise for a little while to-day, and I'm going to get up to-morrow. Oh, Norah, it is nice of you to have come to see me again. Wouldn't you rather be out of doors with the others?"

Norah shook her head, smiling.

" They're gardening again for dear life, under Pat's most capable generalship," she reported, " and your nice Nurse Glover is helping them. They'll all be coming to see you after tea. I thought I'd take a holiday this afternoon, for a change."

It was just a fortnight since the episode of the Fair, and Andrea was definitely on the road to convalescence. Norah, who had been over to see her on several week-day evenings, was beginning to realize that she had a lot in common with Lady Royston's brilliant, but irresponsible grandchild. They both loved books, for one thing, and Norah had helped to keep Andrea supplied, as soon as she began to demand to be allowed to read again. Somehow, good friends though she was and always would be, with Pat and the others, Norah had missed companionship to a certain extent, because she was a good deal quicker-brained and more imaginative than the other Marigolds, and could, whenever she chose, outstrip them mentally. In Andrea she had met a match—and she was inclined to suspect sometimes, rather more than a match. One had to get up extremely early in the morning, she was beginning to realize, if one wanted to catch Andrea napping!

On the present occasion, however, Andrea was in a serious mood. Her heart-shaped face looked nearly as white as the pillow peering out from the scatter of thick, dark brown hair, and her big brown eyes were brooding and speculative.

" What have you been thinking about?" Nora questioned curiously.

" Oh, awfully practical things," Andrea assured her. " First of all, I've been wondering if I would make a good Guide. What do you think—do you think I would?"

Norah blinked.

" I've never really thought about it," she admitted, " not since you said you couldn't possibly be one."

" I couldn't belong to an ordinary company, and I don't suppose I'd ever have the patience to get badges —except maybe Musician's," Andrea reflected. " But you don't belong to a company either, at present, and you don't seem to bother much about badges, any of you. It's *being* a Guide I want to know about."

" But why? What makes you want to be one, I mean?" Norah was puzzled.

Andrea frowned. Her hand stole down and fidgeted with the strings of her violin, so that they gave out faint, plaintive cheepings, like the notes of a very small bird.

" I don't know," she said slowly. Then, in a rush, the colour flooding into her face: " You'll think I'm a lunatic, I expect—but ever since I was little—before I can remember, even, Mummie and Daddie and Grannie and everybody have thought of me first and foremost as a musician. I was just born one. I couldn't be anything else and I don't want to be, but sometimes it's awfully lonely and rather frightening to feel that

maybe it's the music inside you people mind about—
not you yourself, at all. I tried to explain to Grannie,
the first night I was here, and although she laughed at
me at first, she said, I was all wrong if I thought people
wouldn't—well, like me, and be friends, without my
music. She said she betted you all would, and it'd
be jolly good for me to take my chance and knock
about like an ordinary person for a bit."

"Well, we do like you," Norah suddenly smiled
and added, "most awfully."

Andrea nodded, and the odd puckish look came to
her face for a moment.

"I purposely wouldn't let you hear me play. You
never have, even now, Norah."

"No, but the others told me about you," Norah
said soberly. "Anyway, I don't see it makes much
difference, really, Andy. I mean, your music's only
a bit of you, even if it's the most important bit, isn't
it?"

"Yes," Andrea agreed. "That's what I've been
thinking. It's always mattered so much, though, that
I haven't thought a lot about the other bits. It's not
good enough to have only one thing in life you can
do well. Daddie's said that to me often, but I was so
full of my training and my success I couldn't see it
myself, until now. I'm older than either you or Pat,
but neither of you would have let the three kids in for
trouble like I did the Saturday I got ill—would you?
You'd have remembered to think ahead, and 'be
prepared'. Well, it was lucky for me that I was the

one who got ill through it. I'd have felt much worse
if one of them had. But now I want to be like you and
Pat, and learn to keep my head screwed on more. I
think if I was a Guide it would help. It does, doesn't
it?"

"Yes." Norah was quite serious now. "It does,
Andrea. You see—one doesn't bleat all the time about
the Promise and the Laws, but they're always *there*,
somehow, in the background, something to measure
life up against, a standard to go by."

"That's what I mean." Andrea nodded. "That's
what I'd like to have. Look here, can't I be enrolled
as a Lone Guide? Mary's mother says she thinks that
would be the best way."

"Yes, I expect you could be, easily," Norah agreed.
"I'll write and ask Captain what we shall have to do
to get you enrolled. Oh, Andrea, I'm glad—it'll be
fun!"

Andrea drew her violin up on to her knees and
nursed it there, hugging it with both arms.

"Norah, there was something else. Another idea
I had."

"What was that?" Norah wondered a little anxiously
if quite so many ideas were good for a person still ill
enough to have a nurse looking after her and Dr.
Ormonde calling every day.

"Well——" Andrea hesitated. "Maybe you'll
think it's interference. That's why I asked about
being a Guide first—because if I am one, you'll sort
of feel more like letting me share in things."

" But, Andy, we always wanted you to share—how do you mean?"

" It's about your idea of helping old Ellie to get a house," Andrea confided.

" Yes?" Norah queried.

" I've thought two things. The first was that maybe a *caravan* would be much easier to get, and to move than that hut you were telling me about. You see, I really do know lots of gipsies and most of them like caravans best to live in. They're awfully dry, standing right up high off the ground on wheels—and then, if you want to move, it's so easy—just borrow a horse, if you don't own one, and there you are. I got the idea when I was at Fransham. You see, that gipsy man took us to his camp, when he was going to drive us home. I noticed then that they'd put a caravan out, away from the actual camping ground, with a notice ' For Sale ' on it. It was a nice one—almost new. I asked him about it a bit—not much, because I felt so funny—and he said it belonged to his brother, but they'd bought a motor lorry and didn't need it any more. What d'you think?"

" I don't know," Norah considered the proposition. " It sounds a good idea—so good, I can't imagine why none of us ever thought of it before. Did you ask him what it would cost?"

" No," Andrea admitted, " but I don't expect it would be as much as the hut."

Norah sighed.

" We haven't even begun to get enough money

for that—so the caravan is sure to be sold before we can bid for it," she complained. "Oh, money is a nuisance!"

"That's the other bit of my idea," Andrea told her, triumphantly, "the bit I didn't like to suggest if I wasn't to be a Guide, in case you thought it was cheek. You know, Norah, if I'm going to be a Guide it'll be quite fair for me to help, won't it? No, don't get mad until you hear how I mean—I mean, we could give a garden fête one Saturday, and have lots of things, side shows, and guessing games and things, and serve teas, and then after tea I'd give a recital. I know it sounds swank, but people *do* come when I play. In Paris they sold out all the tickets for my last concert within an hour of the box-office opening. So, if we had some placards printed, and put a notice in the local paper, as well, I expect we'd get more people to the fête than if I didn't play. That's why I suggest playing, see?"

"Andy, you *are* a sweet person," impulsively Norah bent forward and laid her hand on Andrea's. "Of course, it's a lovely idea, and I'm certain it'll work, but I don't think many terribly famous people would suggest it, and you are just terribly famous, I'm beginning to discover."

"Oh, rats!" Andrea flushed, and to hide a sudden shyness tucked the violin under her chin and began to play an odd, wistful little air. Sunset light, flooding through the long window, touched her hair with bronze gleams and Norah smiled to herself.

" What are you thinking?" Andrea asked softly.

" Only that French Marigolds are brown colour," Norah told her.

Andrea's eyes caught the smile.

" Meaning——?"

" Oh, just that you *belong*, that's all."

CHAPTER XVIII

The Wishing Well

" How would you like to take this afternoon as a real holiday?" Lady Royston inquired, looking quizzically from one to another of the Marigolds, determinedly getting out tools, on the blazing hot June afternoon which followed Andrea's conversation with Norah.

" We'd like it a lot. A whole tremendous, enormous lot," Norah said promptly.

The patrol grinned, damply warm, after the long walk up the hill, and all secretly just a trifle tired of weeding, hoeing, staking and hedge-clipping. Only small Mary's eyes were doubtful, fixed on Lady Royston's face with an anxious expression.

" I've some plants to see about at the Abbey Nurseries at Chiddingley," Lady Royston explained briskly. " It's a very pretty place, and if you'd like to come, we can have tea over there, and drive home by way of Fransham Common. I understand you and Andrea have an errand at the gipsy camp there, Norah?"

Norah nodded.

" That would be perfectly lovely. Will Andrea be able to come?"

" Of course. The drive will do her good on such a lovely day. I wonder if your mother would care to come, Mary? Or would you rather stay behind and have tea with her here?" Lady Royston asked kindly.

Mary hesitated a fraction of a second. Then she said slowly:

" It'd be awfully nice if she could come. She'd love it for her last day in the country, I think. But will we be too many in the car?"

" No, I don't think so. A bit of a squeeze doesn't hurt small sardines like you," Lady Royston told her. The old lady's eyes were suddenly very kind, as they often were when she looked at the Marigold's odd little recruit.

Bravely, Mary smiled back at her. In some queer way, the two understood each other. Lady Royston realized, as she had realized from the beginning, that though it had been a delirious treat to Mary to have her mother within reach for three whole weeks, she was going to pay for it heavily, now that there really was no reason why Andrea should have a nurse any longer. Mary, however, meant to do her paying cheerfully, and Lady Royston respected her for it.

The patrol, though they did not say much, sympathized with Mary wholeheartedly. Little Nurse Glover, thin, dark-haired, dark-eyed, with a quick capable manner, an unfailing sense of humour, and an equally unfailing fund of common sense, had proved a real asset at Stone House, the three weeks she had been there. Quite how anybody so neat, dainty and well-groomed came to be the mother of Mary, with her sprooky hair, untidy clothes and invariable smut or ink-streaked physiognomy, was a problem however.

On the present occasion, no sooner had they gathered on the shallow steps outside the house, waiting for the car, than Mary's mother swooped down on her, and after a brief, but satisfying hug, carried her off to the bathroom to be combed and brushed, and have a hole in her stocking mended.

" You're a disgrace, my child, you look as if you've been pulled through at least six hedges backwards," she told her. " Why didn't you mend that hole before you started?"

" Oh, I don't know, I never saw it," Mary answered placidly.

Biddie, kicking her heels against the big iron-scraper, said thoughtfully:

" Mary always says that."

" What?" Patsy queried.

" ' I never saw it '," Biddie quoted. " She said it when Miss Rollins rowed her for coming to class with a dirty face last week. I wonder if she *really* doesn't see?"

" I don't suppose she ever looks," Patsy said judicially. " She's a careless little baggage, our Mary."

But Biddie, continuing to kick the scraper monotonously, seemed lost in thought.

.   .   .   .

" That caravan isn't sold, Grannie. Mr. Hearn's let us look all over it, and he says he'll wait a month, if we like, as it's for an ' old ancient person of the real Romany sort '. He's ever so nice. It costs eighteen pounds. I don't think that's a lot, do you?"

Andrea, balancing herself on one foot on the running board of Lady Royston's big car, thrust her head in at the window, interrupting, without apology, an earnest conversation that had been in progress between her Grandmother and Nurse Glover.

Lady Royston, rather startled, looked up. The car was parked on the side of the main road that runs across Fransham Common. In the distance, the caravans and huts of the gipsy camps showed on the edge of a little wood, looking romantic and homely in the glow of the warm, sun-filled evening. Mary had come back with Andrea, but the rest of the patrol were missing.

" You've been very quick, Andrea. Where are the others?" Lady Royston queried suspiciously.

" Over there still, Grannie. Mr. Hearn says there's a wishing well—a really truly one—in that wood. I thought maybe you'd like to see it, too. He says the water goes down if what you wish isn't coming true and stays up if it is, so you can tell what your luck is going to be. Do come." Andrea was enthusiastic.

" Hmph!" Lady Royston snorted. " The nonsense people make you believe, Andrea, really, you might be five instead of fifteen!"

However, by dint of a little coaxing, she was easily persuaded to consent to the expedition. As the four of them walked across the grassy track, through the young, budding heather plants, Andrea slipped her hand through Nurse Glover's arm.

" Has Grannie asked you—about our idea, and the cottage?" she asked.

Mary looked up in a startled way.

" What idea?" she asked, before her mother could answer.

" We were just discussing it, when you interrupted us," Lady Royston rebuked her grandchild's impetuosity. " Mary, Andrea and I both feel you and your mother want a home of your own. Now, the Lodge at the south gate of Stone House has been empty for six months, because I wanted to have someone really reliable whom I could trust living there, but I must find a tenant soon, for it's going to go to rack and ruin if I don't. Andrea suggested Mrs. Glover might be willing to take care of it for me, and to become our District Nurse."

" But—but—you mean Mummie *live* there?" Mary asked breathlessly.

" You too, Mary. You could easily bicycle into school every day. You could have the bike I grew out of last time I was at Stone House," Andrea told her.

" Oh, Mummie—can we? Will you? Oh, Mummie, *do*." Mary begged incoherently.

" My chicken, can't you guess how much I want to?" Mrs. Glover told her quickly. " But we mustn't count on it—not yet. You see, there are a lot of things to settle."

" What sort of things?" Andrea challenged. " You

know you want to come. You'd just adore to. *I* know how much you love the country, though I've only known you three weeks—and Grannie can get you the job of District Nurse for absolutely certain sure. We found out before we asked you."

"Yes, but, dear, I've got a contract signed, to a Nursing Home in London, to work as a private nurse."

"But, Mummie——" Mary clasped her mother's wrist with both hands. "Mummie, that ends in August. Couldn't we start living in the cottage then, when you're free?"

"If Lady Royston wouldn't mind the delay," Mrs. Glover began, with some hesitation.

"I think that could be arranged," Lady Royston said reassuringly. "In fact," as she caught the desperate appeal in Mary's eyes, "I'm certain it can. Now, go on, you two, you lead the way. Nurse and I can talk over the details together."

"Oh, Andrea, Andrea darling, you are a witch. I always knew you were. The first minute I saw you." Mary, utterly breathless with excitement, scurried ahead as directed, keeping difficult pace with Andrea's long legs.

"And how did you know that?" Andrea inquired.

"'Cos of your hair," Mary said, surprisingly. "I read in a book that 'a witch may be known by her hair, which is straight for three or four inches, and then begins to curl, like a waterfall which comes down smoothly, and then rebounds on the neck'. Yours does just that."

Andrea laughed outright.

"'Witches, warlocks and gipsies soon ken ae the ither'," she quoted. "*I've* read *The Gipsy Anthology*, Mary, what are you, a warlock? You must be, for you aren't a witch and I don't believe you're a gipsy."

They were still chuckling over the joke, when they rejoined the rest of the patrol on the edge of the little wood of fir trees.

"You have been a long time," Pixie complained. "We've been right through, and seen the well. It's ever so creepy."

"Mr. Hearn's waiting for us there. Biddie's talking to him about her everlasting herbs," Patsy announced.

"We were bored, so we came to meet you. Mary, child, you look as if you'd had your wish already. What's she so excited about, for mercy's sake, Andy?" Norah queried.

By the time they had explained, Lady Royston and Mrs. Glover had come up.

"Now, where's this wonderful hocus-pocus place, and what is it we have to do?" Andrea's Grandmother demanded, sarcastically. Nobody minded her sarcasm, because they knew quite well that at heart she was always as excited as they were about any new adventure.

"This way—I'll show you," Pixie volunteered, skipping ahead, through the tall green plants of the dog mercury, and the hooded "lords and ladies" that fringed the path.

"It's ever such a queer place, truly it is," Norah repeated.

Even Lady Royston was inclined to agree, when they finally reached the little, mossy hollow, where, surrounded by a circle of dark firs, the well lay, very deep and quiet, within its parapet of worn, grey-stone blocks.

" That's Roman work, if I'm not much mistaken," Lady Royston said, after examining the stone carefully. " Odd, that one's never heard of this before. It must be very old, in any case."

" Among us, we call it Cæsar's well, lady." The tall gipsy, who had come to Andrea's call, on the Saturday of the storm, stepped forward, cap in hand. " Hundreds of years old, it is, and so deep no stone ever touches the bottom. But if you drops a pebble, just a small, little stone, and drops your wish with it, you'll see the water rise or fall, just as the wish is to come to you or not, as I was telling the pretty young ladies."

Lady Royston chuckled.

" Well, give me a stone. Here, Norah, you try first, let's see if you're to be lucky!"

Norah, enjoying the dramatic possibilities of the game, obediently took the small pebble the gipsy handed her.

" I wish——" she began, but he stopped her.

" Tell your wishes to the water, my lady dear; don't speak them aloud, not before the pebble's fallen."

" All right." Norah leaned over the parapet. Far below, a circle of water reflected the patch of blue sky between the trees. With a quick, determined gesture, she let the stone go and it plopped into the water gently.

"Why, it *is* rising, look, there are quite waves on it!" she exclaimed a moment later.

"Yes, it really does rise. What fun! I bet it's what they call an 'optical illusion' though. Let me try now," Andrea begged. A moment later, she gave a little grunt of disgust. "How sickening! I wished Mrs. Glover and Mary could come to the Lodge *at once*, next week, and look what's happening!"

The Marigolds, their heads reflected in silhouette, peered at the falling level of the water.

"How awfully queer." Nurse Glover was intrigued. "May I try?"

As the water rose again she laughed delightedly; rather a relieved laugh.

"Well, it's going to be all right in the end, Andrea. Of course, I wished we should come to the Lodge some day."

"Oh, Mummie, now you've bagged my wish!" Mary was indignant. "I've nothing left to wish for. I can't think of a single other thing."

Biddie's observant suggestion that the rise and fall came alternately, proved incorrect. The water obligingly rose for her and Pixie. When Lady Royston dropped her pebble, on the other hand, there was no appreciable movement either way.

"It's stuck," Norah said interestedly.

"The magic's run out," Andrea suggested.

"It's tired of playing," Pat remarked flippantly.

Mary, looking at Lady Royston, said accusingly:
" You didn't wish at all!"

As they all turned away, laughing and teasing her
in the attempt to find out if this was really the case,
small Mary hesitated.

She had not had her wish—and now she had thought
of one—one she didn't want the others to ask her
about. Of course, they didn't, any of them, really
believe—it was only for fun. Surreptitiously she
dropped a pebble. *Plop* it went, loudly in the quiet
wood.

" Ooh, Mary's wished, and her wish is coming
true!" Pixie shrilled.

Flushed, Mary drew back from the well-head. She
looked thoroughly guilty for a moment, then she
laughed, as if at a very funny joke.

" It's not true," she said. " I only wished it for
fun."

" What was it?" Biddie asked.

But Mary would only shake her head.

" Something that can't ever happen. The well's
clever, but you *can* catch it out," she affirmed.

CHAPTER XIX

"Yo-ho-ho, and a Bottle of Rum"

" Patsy Ormonde, just tell me one thing; could we have had a better day for a garden fête if we'd ordered it in advance, and chosen our own pattern?" Norah, busy tin-tacking bunting to the edge of a wooden garden bench, which was to act as a stall, on the terrace outside Stone House, paused, and looked out across the garden, glowing with July colours in the early morning sunshine.

" Or a better place?" Patsy added gratefully. " We are lucky, really."

Norah chuckled.

" For a patrol that's got no company, and no officers and no anything, we seem to have had a pretty good run for our money lately," she admitted. Banging in the last tack vigorously, she added, " It's Lady Royston's fault. She's been an angel to us, all through. I only wish we could ever tell her as big a ' thank you ' as we feel, for everything."

" Well," Patsy shook out a cloth and spread it on the table with precision, " I'm not sure she wants to be thanked. Maybe it's true what Mary says her mother said—that Lady Royston's been thankful to

155

have us, to make friends for Andrea. She said Andrea
had never enjoyed a holiday so much before. She's
usually bored and restless after about a week."

"Andrea does get bored easily," Norah admitted.
"I've noticed that. She just hates it, when we're out
hiking all day, if I give her any of the dull jobs to do,
like collecting wood. But she does do them, now,
which she wouldn't at first."

"You'll miss her an awful lot when she goes home,
won't you?" Patsy asked, a trifle sadly.

Her leader looked up, and their eyes met. Norah
rose impulsively and went round the table until she
stood by Patsy's side.

"Not jealous, you donkey, are you?" she asked
kindly.

Patsy shook her head.

"Not really, only, sometimes, I wish I could be
clever and brilliant and quick, like you two. I'm so
stodgy, Norah, beside you both. And I do know it."

"Well, it's a jolly good thing for the Marigolds
you supply them with a bit of ballast, now and then,
that's all!" Norah told her emphatically. "I reckon
the pirates' long-boat would be apt to turn turtle if
you didn't weight it down occasionally, with your
'stodginess' as you call it. *I* call it your common
sense. As for Andrea, she'd land us in all manner of
scrapes, if she had her way. I say, Patsy, I do wish
she could come to school for a bit with us all. She
was talking about it the other day, and she's awfully
keen. She says she's never wanted to before, because

she thought it would be dull, and she wouldn't make friends—but we'd see her through, wouldn't we?"

"Rather," Patsy agreed enthusiastically. She glanced at her watch. "Goodness! Do you realize it's already nearly ten, and we've only done this one stall? If we gossip, we shall lose all the advantage of having got here early. We've loads to do—all the tea tables to set, and the sports-ground to lay out, and the chairs to arrange for Andrea's recital. Come on, let's hurry. By now the kids ought to have finished labelling the plants in the herb garden. Let's collect the whole patrol and start by fixing up the games. I'm sure it'll take us ages."

The patrol had entered into Andrea's idea of a garden fête, the proceeds to be devoted to "The Marigold Patrol Funds", with a will and also with a considerable expenditure of ingenuity.

They had decided that the afternoon should begin with games and sports for everybody—energetic ones for the younger visitors, more sedate for the elderly.

"We can't possibly afford proper prizes—so we'll give funny ones," Norah had decreed, and Lady Royston had suggested that queer little birds and beasts, made from pine cones, gathered on the estate, and painted by hand, would fit the occasion nicely.

The Marigolds had, accordingly, raided the wood for cones and the barnyard for feathers, and spent some delightful evenings with glue and paint pots, in Mr. Hewlett's workshop, after school. Patsy, who was dainty with any kind of craft work, had evolved a way of making really delightful buttonholes out of the smaller cones and dried oak-apples, mounted on wire, round which she afterwards twisted green silk.

" Those we'll sell—and little bunches of flowering herbs, too, for luck. Pixie can have them on a tray," Norah suggested.

They had tried, under the instructions of a very old, musty-smelling book Mary had discovered, to make " pomanders " of dried oranges, stuffed with herbs. These, however, had not been a success. After two had gone mouldy, and they had discovered a large family of earwigs in a third, they had let the matter drop, deciding philosophically that the Elizabethan lady who wrote the recipe probably had a different kind of orange to begin on.

Now the day was actually upon them, there seemed to be a great many things left to be done, by way of preparation, in spite of all the care they had expended beforehand, and when, at a quarter to one, Lady Royston called them in to get ready for lunch, they were hot, dishevelled, and inclined to be fussed.

" Suppose only about two people come after all, shan't we feel silly?" Biddie groaned.

" Suppose millions of people come, whatever shall we do to keep them amused?" Patsy countered.

" I've told everybody in my form about it. I expect they'll all come, because I said it was going to be too simply thrilling," Pixie boasted.

" Well, I can't personally see it's going to be thrilling

at all," Andrea snapped nervously. " I wish to goodness we'd never begun on it now."

" Don't worry, it'll be all over by this time to-
morrow, even if we have all made fools of ourselves,"
Norah comforted her, with more philosophy than
tact.

Lady Royston, presiding behind the big veal and
ham pie at the head of the old-fashioned dinner table,
said nothing, but served out helpings generously, and
saw to it the jugs of home-made lemonade were passed
round. The best remedy for " stage-fright " before
such an occasion as the present, was, she considered,
a good square meal.

This proved to be the case, and when, after lunch,
the entire patrol retired upstairs to wash and change,
they were in much better spirits. They had decided
that, as the wearing of uniform was going to entail
a great deal of explanation beforehand in order to
gain the necessary permission, they would dress as
pirates.

" We *are* a pirate crew, so we may as well look like
one," Norah had backed the suggestion, and added,
honestly, " it's about the easiest fancy-dress to do—
top-boots, and shorts, and open-necked shirts—we
only need brilliant coloured handkerchiefs round our
heads and waists, and a black patch or two, and p'raps
a few skulls and crossbones—they always look effec-
tive!"

" Andrea can't be a pirate for her recital," Mary
had objected.

" Why not? I'd love to be!" Andrea herself had protested.

" It isn't sort of—sort of dignified enough, is it, Norah?" Mary had argued.

" Well, I tell you what I'll do," Andrea capitulated. " If you'll let me be a pirate to begin with I'll change before my recital and put on my real Hungarian gipsy dress. Will that do? It's one Daddy bought for me last time we went to Bourgenland and it's ever so quaint and pretty."

To this they all finally agreed.

There is something exhilarating about " dressing-up " even to the most unimaginative person. By the time six pirates swaggered down the stairs and strode resolutely out on to the terrace in front of Stone House, the Marigold Patrol had decided that it was looking forward to its own garden fête, after all.

" Now, you know your jobs," Norah reminded them. " Patsy is on duty at the Lodge gate, to charge admission and sell tea tickets. Pixie can direct people where things are, as well as sell buttonholes. Mary is going to be my orderly and help me with the sports. Andrea is taking charge of the fish pond and the other quiet games, and Biddie of the herb garden. At four o'clock I shall blow a ' rally ' call on my whistle, and everybody will come and help with teas."

" Except me," Mary reminded her. " I'm to take Patsy's place, in case people come late."

" Yes, I'd forgotten. We must have somebody at the gate until five o'clock, or even half-past. After

that we'll risk putting William in charge. He's promised to be there," Norah recapitulated. " Good-luck,
everybody, and if anything happens that you can't
cope with, blow an S.O.S. and we'll all come to the
rescue!"

" I expect some fat old lady'll fall in the fish pond,
and I shan't be able to rescue her, so do come quick
if you hear me call," Andrea suggested flippantly.

"If the Queen comes, or the Chief Guide arrives,
I'll signal for help," Patsy promised.

Norah chuckled.

" You might send us a warning ' toot ' if Miss
Nesbitt and Captain arrive," she suggested. " After
all, we put the announcement on the school notice
board and one never knows."

By three o'clock no doubts remained that the
Marigolds' fête was going to be a success. The gardens
of Stone House were famous in the neighbourhood,
and quite a number of local people were only too glad
of an excuse to visit them on such a beautiful summer
afternoon. St. Bridget's, also, intrigued by what they
considered the " cheek " of the patrol, in carrying on
so flourishingly, in spite of circumstances, turned out
in full force. Almost all the Cornflowers and Heathers
arrived together, having come out on the same train,
and Madge and Alice were generous in their praise.

" I think you're marvellous," Madge told Norah,
enthusiastically. " I'd never have had the nerve to
plan a show like this. Isn't there anything we can do
to help?"

" Yes, lots," Norah told them promptly, " be angels, will you, and enter for some of the mad items on this sports list, the banana race, and the treasure hunt, and things? It'll encourage outside people to join in, if you do."

The Guides found this task a most pleasant one, and soon the big meadow where the patrol had organized the sports, was thronged with a much amused crowd of spectators and performers, and laughter and clapping could be heard on all sides, as the more ridiculous of the items took place. Numbers of " grown-ups " entered for the games, encouraged by the enthusiasm of the younger set. The sight of large and moderately elderly fathers of families, lying flat on the ground in pairs, their hands tied behind them, gobbling up a skinned banana from opposite ends, with tremendous concentration, left Norah almost too helpless to continue her duties as master of the ceremonies. However, the essence of such entertainments lies in keeping things moving, and she hastened to explain the rules of the treasure hunt, directly she could make herself heard again.

Mary, scuttling happily from point to point in the grounds, reported that Andrea had quite a crowd fishing for bobbing corks with cotton and bent pins up on the lily pond, and some people were playing tortoise croquet, and others thoroughly enjoying a version of Kim's game that the patrol had adapted, in which one had to remember where in the grounds certain trees, flowers or vegetables were to be found.

" Biddie's having a lovely time in the herb garden. People are thrilled with it. Pixie's getting them all to go down there, by showing them her buttonholes and 'splaining about how interesting it is, and how we did every bit of it ourselves," Mary reported.

Mentally, Norah put up a prayer that Pixie might not be showing off to too frightful an extent, and let it go at that. It seemed the only way.

CHAPTER XX

A Garden of Sweet Herbs

" You must have had fun—really great fun—resurrecting this place. I can't think how you found out the names of so many old fashioned plants, let alone their uses. Did Lady Royston help you?" Miss Nesbitt asked Biddie in the friendliest of tones.

Biddie, still in her pirate costume, gulped. It really was just her luck, she reflected, to be in charge of the herb garden when the head mistress of St. Bridget's herself appeared! She looked up shyly at the tall, pleasant figure, in the pretty, cool dress of blue and white flowered silk. Somehow, Miss Nesbitt did not seem so very frightening, here, in the shady open air. She looked somehow younger, and much more like the Guider Biddie knew she had been, than like the autocratic organizer who was, slowly but surely, pulling up the standard of a big and flourishing school. Biddie, quick to notice such things at any time, saw that there were shadows under her eyes and little lines at the corners of her mouth, now. The term had been long and trying, and the strain had made the young head mistress tired, in spite of her gallant bearing.

" Won't you sit down on the grass seat for a bit and rest?" she suggested. " This is ever such a resty sort of place, Miss Nesbitt. I think it's the lovely smell of thyme and mint and verbena all mixed up together, don't you?"

" Lavender and rosemary, too——" Miss Nesbitt sniffed appreciatively, sinking down on the bank Biddie had indicated, with a little sigh of relief.

The sunken herb garden, where the Marigolds had worked so hard, lay beyond the lily pond, and was surrounded by a most rampagious hedge of sweet briar, which, un-pruned for years, had grown both tall and thick at its own wild will, and was now covered with shallow, fragile pink and crimson blossoms. It shut the place into a cool and fragrant seclusion, and from its roots the turf banks sloped down to a plot, perhaps a hundred feet by fifty, divided into four beds by a crossway path of worn and mellow brick. Within these beds grew the herbs, now tidily staked, weeded and named.

" You haven't answered my question," Miss Nesbitt reminded Biddie quietly. " How did you learn about all this?"

" Old Ellie taught us—Ellie's a gipsy—and some of it Mary and Andrea and Norah got out of books, and some Daddy taught me," Biddie explained. " We really started to weed this patch as a sort of ' thank you ' to Lady Royston, but we've had a lovely time doing it."

" I'm sure you have." Miss Nesbitt let her glance rest on the elder tree that stood in one corner, sweeping the ground with its flat trusses of cream-coloured flower. " By the way, Miss Blagrove tells me you are going in for the Patrol Competition. How are you finding time to work for that as well as do all this gardening, and organizing of fêtes and so forth?"

Her eyes, deep blue and very piercing, suddenly rested keenly on Biddie's face. Biddie drew a deep breath.

" We aren't," she admitted. " Not as a patrol, anyway. We've somehow got a feeling that if we all go on and learn interesting things together, the rest'll, well, sort of come. At least, I think that's what Norah and Patsy think," she added rather confusedly.

" Humph! From what I remember of my young days such things as morse had a way of *going* unless I kept on practising them," Miss Nesbitt suggested humorously, " but perhaps you have much better memories."

" Oh, Norah says *those* sort of things are our ' private responsibility '," Biddie said calmly. " Once Guides has taught us a thing it's our choice whether we remember or forget it. After all, we all had to learn to walk and talk, she says, but our parents don't go *on* teaching us, now. She says she thinks most Guide companies waste a lot of time practising things the Guides could practise alone, and that's why they get bored."

" I see," Miss Nesbitt nodded.

Biddie wondered rather anxiously if she really did see, and wished devoutly that the task of making her had fallen to one of the others. She did not feel she was good at explaining. She rather thought she must have said something to annoy the head mistress, for Miss Nesbitt got up, without another word, and began to walk to the little rustic gate which closed the entrance to the garden. She paused once or twice and bent to read the labels so painstakingly printed with indelible pencil.

" Ground ivy—for coughs.

" Loosestrife—stops bleeding.

" Balm—use dried in pot-pourri.

" Borage—flavouring for salads, or cooling summer drinks.

" Germander—helps rheumatism."

At the gate she paused, and looked back at the green place, dappled with splashes of evening sunshine. It seemed to Biddie that, in some odd way, she was appreciating it more fully than any of the people who, earlier in the afternoon, had gone into noisy raptures about it.

Suddenly her eyes came back to Biddie's face and she smiled—a smile so beautiful that it startled the younger Marigold, who had always thought of her before as rather a stern, forbidding person.

" ' Very delightful is a garden of green herbs '," she quoted softly. " You're a lucky patrol to find your job in restoring something so restful and so sweet."

Then, as Biddie flushed with pleasure at such understanding praise, she added thoughtfully:

" Dignity — simplicity — graciousness — the Eliza-bethan women, who planned such gardens as these, had all those things, and yet they were thoroughly efficient and hard-headed people, as much on the spot as any of us who make such a graceless rush of life. We might do much worse than learn a little poise from them."

Before Biddie could reply, the faint, insistent calling of a patrol leader's whistle from the direction of the house roused them both.

" That means it's nearly six o'clock and Andrea's recital is going to begin," Biddie explained, and added rather shyly, " will you come and listen to it, Miss Nesbitt? Andrea does really play very well."

Miss Nesbitt smiled.

" You needn't tell me that, Biddie. I've heard Andrea Jokai play at the Albert Hall. We're very, very lucky to have such a treat this afternoon. Is her recital to be in the house?"

" No, on the lawn we call ' Fountain Lawn '," Biddie explained. " We didn't think it was fair on Lady Royston to have people tramping in and out of the house, and Andrea doesn't mind playing out of doors. We moved the piano out this morning, and Mr. Briton, who plays the church organ, practised with her then. I hope it'll be all right," Biddie said a little nervously.

Without further talk she led the way, through the rose garden and the long alleys of clipped box to the smooth, green lawn, surrounded by tall yew hedges and formal flower beds, where people were gathering, shepherded by the now warm and weary, but well-satisfied " pirates " responsible for the long and most successful afternoon.

A little breeze ruffled through the big oak tree on the far side of the lawn, under which the piano had been established, and the warm scent of heliotrope filled the evening air. Scattered about, some on chairs and benches, some sitting on the grass, the audience gathered steadily.

" There must be nearly three hundred people here, Norah," Patsy remarked in rather awed tones, after a frantic attempt at counting. " I say, I do hope Andrea will play well. She's frightfully, frightfully nervous. She was almost crying when she went in to change."

" Oh, she'll be all right," Norah prophesied. " Real musicians almost always feel like that before a concert, I believe."

Andrea, indeed, when she walked through the gap in the natural green wall, just as the stable clock chimed six, looked perfectly self-possessed, though she was rather paler than usual.

" That's not a *gipsy* dress," Pixie complained in a whisper of protest.

" It is—the Hungarian sort," Norah reassured her.

" It's very pretty, anyway," Biddie said decisively.

The wide skirted, tight bodiced frock which Andrea wore was made of velvet, the colour of old parchment, sewn all over with a heavy pattern in gold thread and turquoises and sequins. The sleeves were also very full, caught into little cuffs at the wrist, and made of soft, turquoise-blue silk. She had scarlet leather slippers, and round her dark hair a crown of worked gold leaves.

She smiled encouragingly at little Mr. Briton, who looked pink and perspiring behind his spectacles; tuned her violin carefully, and began to play.

She had chosen a programme of gracious, old world music, that fitted the place and hour. Haydn, Mozart, a queer little cradle-song of Purcel, and then, soul satisfying and complete, a Beethoven symphony, arranged for single violin.

" Oh, it's lovely, lovely, lovely," Mary murmured rapturously, as the shattering applause rose and fell, and rose again.

" I think she's marvellous," Patsy said dazedly. " I knew she could play well, but—I see now why people go mad about violin music. I never did see before."

" Hush, she's going to give an encore," Norah warned.

Andrea, tossing the loose hair back from her shoulders, stepped forward and smiled at her audience.

" I should like to end this concert by playing you a piece of music called ' Transylvanian Melody '," she said. " The Transylvanian gipsies have many beautiful old tunes, which can still be heard round their camp fires on the Hungarian plains. Someone who knows them well has gathered those tunes together and made them into a sort of story. First it tells of the time when they were oppressed—the words of the song are very sad.

> " Strike whom thou wilt, O God, alas!
>   Enough thy fires have scorched me.
>   Strike down, O God, these walls, for ah!
>   They cannot else surmounted be."

Later, when they were free again, they sang a lovely little cradle song for their children:

> " Little bird of Paradise,
>   Do the work of Jesu Christ;
>   Go by sea, go by land,
>   Ever by God's holy hand."

There are dances, too, the czardas, particularly, also the mazurka and the wedding dances, and finally there is the blessing of the gipsy, which he gives you when your roads divide:

> " God make thee both a branch and flower;
>   May the Lord send us all a happy hour."

While she was speaking Andrea looked over the heads of the people. Her eyes met those of the Marigolds, with an expression they could not interpret—it was almost as though no one else were there at all —as though she played for them, and for them alone.

As her bow came down across the strings, and the wild, heart-shaking melody of the most pathetic of all the Zigeuna songs rang out across the quiet English garden, Norah thought that she understood. There was something in the gipsy music as it rose and fell, stormy and pleading, or mysteriously, elusively sweet, that belonged to the open air and the green gloom of the woods, to wide skies, and open roads, and the adventure of living. The wild whirl of the czardas, the tinkling, clinking prettiness of the wedding dance, excited her. Then came again a hint of the prisoner's song, and last, very plaintive and haunting, a little refrain that repeated itself again and again, dying fainter and fainter, as if into the distance. She rubbed her hand quickly over her eyes, and turned away, as the applause broke like a hail storm. Slipping out through the gap in the hedge, she made for the house. Andrea would be coming in, almost at once, to change, she knew. She felt she must speak to her, must ask her now, at once, just why she had played that tune—what it meant?

In the shadow of the trees she ran against the scarecrow figure of old Ellie, leaning on her stick. The gipsy's face was flushed, her hands quivering.

"Mishto! Mishto! Brava, brava!" she exclaimed excitedly. "Miss Norah, dear, the young lady's of the true Romany race. 'Tis a Romany Princess's dress she's wearing this day, and right she has, and blessing she has. It's years and it's weary years since I heard the music of my people. Give her old Ellie's blessing, lady dear, and tell her there's great days before her— and before us all, when such as she'll play under the open sky, and no more thought to themselves than if they were simple, ordinary folki."

Norah left her, and urged by an instinct she did

not stop to analyse, raced into the house and upstairs. The door of Andrea's room was shut. She pushed it open and hurried in.

Heedless of her rich dress, and the clean, starched counterpane alike, Andrea lay, face down, on the big bed, sobbing as though her heart would break.

" Andy—dear old thing!" in a moment Norah was beside her. " You're tired. We've let you do far too much, after being ill and all." Then, as Andrea looked up, she asked, startled: " Andy, is anything really wrong?"

Struggling with sobs that shook her still, Andrea nodded.

" A telegram, it came at tea-time, I found it when I came up to dress. Daddie's got moved to another Embassy—and—and—I've got to go home *to-morrow*. They don't say where we are going or anything—just that. Oh, Norah, and I haven't been enrolled, I haven't been anything, and I did so much, so much, *so* much want to be a Guide!"

For a long minute Norah sat very still, her arm round the other girl's shoulders, her face gone scared and grave. Then her grip tightened. With her free hand she unfastened the shining trefoil that held her pirate scarf in place.

" Chief says in the Law, a Guide is a person who *is* honourable, loyal, obedient, kind. I reckon, Andy, you're a Guide now, whether anybody's ever enrolled you or not. I can't enrol you, because I'm not a Captain, but I'm giving you my badge, to prove that you count as one of us, with me. You can wear it always, if you want to, as long as it's where it doesn't show to ordinary people. You'll always be a Marigold and we'll always be tremendously proud, because you are one, and," her voice broke, but she swallowed the lump in her throat and went on bravely, " and some day, Andy, you'll come back, and we'll have a proper enrolment for you. Maybe by then we'll have ' made good ' and be a patrol really worth belonging to!"

CHAPTER XXI

The Road to Barham Towers

The first Saturday in August, appointed for the County Patrol Competition, dawned doubtfully, after a week of thunderstorms and broken weather. The Marigolds, gathered outside Dr. Ormonde's house at nine o'clock in the morning, looked at the heavy sky with some anxiety.

" It's going to simply pour, if you ask me?" Patsy predicted pessimistically.

" We didn't!" Norah told her with a grin. " Here, stop prophesying and help me check up our equipment. Have we got it all here?"

" Two groundsheets, two morse flags, one billy-can, one proper first-aid set, one army blanket, one bundle of dry firewood, one clothes line, six yards of blind-cord and twelve tent pegs with mallet. All present, all correct," Patsy announced. " What about personal kit?"

" ' Uniform, tidy and correct '," Norah quoted from her official letter of instructions. " Are you all properly dressed—let me look?"

She inspected her patrol in detail, but, to their satisfaction as well as her own, had absolutely no fault to find. Pixie's skirt was rather shorter than even the regulation shortness for a person of her age, as she had grown considerably since they had worn uniform last, and Biddie's left pocket button seemed rather precariously sewn on, otherwise they all had the smart, trim appearance which is the result of starching and ironing, polishing and brushing with a will. Mary, who had also grown, fitted her St. Bridget's dress and blazer much more adequately than she had done on the day she became a volunteer. She had, obviously, made a valiant effort to be tidy for once. Her face shone from industrious application of a soapy flannel, and her hair, at any rate for the moment, was well scragged and scraped into place, with a new hair-ribbon.

" You'll do." Norah nodded approval, and referred again to the instructions. " Let's see, ' lunch and tea, a mug each, string, pencil and paper, box of matches, clean handkerchief, knife '—all got those?"

" *And* some chalk, *and* a compass, *and* a haversack with a name on it to put things in—not to mention an assortment of safety-pins and a sewing ' hussif '," Biddie checked off the articles on her fingers.

The Marigolds grinned at one another.

They were proud—and not unjustly proud—of their patrol equipment.

" And *what* is it every Guide needs first in a case of accident and emergency?" Norah asked politely.

" Some clean, cold, drinking water!" four voices answered her in chorus.

Norah did a *chasée-and-pas-seule* across the pavement and back again.

"Nobody can say we aren't prepared, whatever the competition proves about our 'Guide general knowledge and intelligence '," she crowed contentedly. "And I flatter myself we don't look like comic hikers in a funny picture paper, in spite of it," she added contentedly.

"Thanks to Lady Royston," Biddie reminded them loyally.

"Yes.   Her idea of sewing little pockets, with elastic at the top, to the inside of one's haversack, to take matches and bandages and all the odd, nobbly things, does improve its figure, when finally packed," Norah agreed, "and I think the notion of a sixpenny flat fruit-drop bottle, covered with felt and with slots on the back to go on one's belt is marvellous too. Big water bottles are so heavy, and the strap pulls one's tie skewifted in no time. But she ought not to have given us these jolly orange mugs, all to match, and the hanks of orange and brown cord, to go on our belts. She honestly spoils us, I feel."

"She said they were a present from Andrea, to bring us luck," Pixie reminded her, and added: " Ooh, I do so wish Andrea was here to-day. Wouldn't it have been much more exciting if she had been?"

"I wonder how she is getting on," Biddie questioned, rather wistfully.

"I've got a letter from her," Norah announced. "It came this morning, from somewhere abroad.   It

was such a scrimmage getting off I haven't read it yet.
We'll read it in the lorry."

" D'you think Jim's going to be late?" Mary asked
anxiously. " The Town Hall clock's striking nine
now."

" P'raps the lorry won't start," Pixie suggested.

" Maybe he's forgotten about us," Biddie put in.

" We've loads of time. The journey won't take
more than a couple of hours and inspection isn't
until two o'clock," Norah reassured them.

" Two hours! Will it take us two whole hours?"
Pixie looked nervous. " D'you think a lorry'll make
me sick, Norah? 'Cos charabancs do."

" They do me, too," Mary remarked placidly. " So
do buses and trains—but it doesn't matter, as long as
we get there, does it?"

" You'll jolly well both sit in front with Jim, and
then you won't even feel sick," Norah told them with
great decision. " One doesn't in the open air—it's
not a bit like charabancs or buses or trains!" There
were moments when she found the younger members
of her patrol decidedly a responsibility.

Further discussion was cut short by the arrival of
Mr. Hewlett's lorry, already loaded with bright yellow
gravel, and Jim Willox, distinctly apologetic, at the
wheel.

" I'm afraid I'm a bit late—but I've been trying to
fix some sort of a contraption to save you getting all
your uniforms messed up with this gravel of mine,"
the big Rover Scout told them. " It's rare messy

stuff and sticks like the dickens. Mr. Hewlett and I have done what's possible with an old tarpaulin, though, and I'm hoping you'll be all right."

" I'm sure we shall," Norah assured him loyally, and added, " we're jolly lucky to get the lift and it was topping of you and Mr. Hewlett to arrange to take your load to-day."

By dint of some shoving and stowing, the three elder Marigolds and their bundle of kit were ensconced at the back, and Pixie and Mary packed into the driving seat with Jim. Very soon they were jolting out of the town and along the big arterial road to Welworth. Jim proved a most entrancing companion to the two youngest Guides. He explained all the switches and gauges on the dash board, let them turn on and off his big fog lights, and showed them exactly what one did when changing gear. They were soon chattering away to him, telling him all the history of their patrol and asking him innumerable questions about the Wolves, Bears and Panthers who had formed his Scout Troup.

As the two small, shrill voices wafted back, through the clatter of the engine, Norah chuckled.

" Not much wrong with them for the rest of the journey. Jim certainly knows how to get on with kids!"

" Read Andrea's letter now, Norah," Biddie begged. " I do so want to know about the place she's gone to."

Norah settled herself more comfortably on the baggage, stuck her back firmly against the side of the lorry, and drew a letter on thin foreign paper out of her pocket.

"She's only at this place for a short holiday," Norah told them. "She says her father hasn't got his new appointment through yet. They think it may be in Italy though. Oh, wouldn't she love that? She's awfully excited at the idea, but she says she'd rather it was in England. She's asked her people to let her come over to boarding school, but they won't, because of her having pleurisy. They say she's too delicate. She says it's very hot, and not so nice as England, but she's liking seeing new places."

"Is that all?" Biddie asked.

"All except that she sends her love to everybody, and says she's sure we'll win to-day and she'll think of us, and will we write and tell her all about it, and how Ellie's caravan's getting on, and if we've finished painting it yet."

They smiled at each other.

"I wish she could see it, just," Patsy sighed. "I'm jolly well going to take some snapshots of it, inside and out as well, next week-end, and send them to her. It's Andy's concert that made us able to buy it and it isn't a bit fair she hasn't been able to share the fun."

Norah, re-reading part of Andrea's letter, was interrupted by two large spots of rain plopping on to it.

"Dash! Here it comes! Macks on, everybody!"

The shower did not last many minutes, and as the

rain stopped the sun came out and gleamed on the shining yellow charlock in the fields through which the lorry was passing.

" Jolly!" Norah shook the wet from the brim of her hat, and sniffed appreciatively. " That's just made everything smell nice, and laid the dust for us. Now it's going to clear up. I say, what a view one gets from these hills. It's the top of the world." She stood up, cautiously, one hand holding to the high tilt of the lorry.

Jim had abandoned the main road, and was taking a short cut of his own to Welworth over a ridge of high, open downland. The white, chalky road ran like a ribbon between the lonely fields, and except for a farm or two nestling in the valley there was not a house in sight. Far behind them, the sun winked along the coast line, and away to the right, almost out of sight, Patsy thought she could make out the spire of Welworth Cathedral.

" I know where we are, we're near Wychborough Beacon. Daddie brought us for a picnic here last year, didn't he, Biddie? In a minute we come out in a place where four roads meet, and then—my goodness —hold on, Norah—look out!"

Before any of them could do anything, and while the scared exclamation was still on Patsy's lips, the accident had happened.

Jim's lorry, gathering speed down the slight dip that led to the cross roads, was travelling fast. A knot of gorse bushes, a good deal thicker and taller than

they appeared at first, obscured the corner. A big
blue saloon car, travelling fast on the London Road,
emerged from behind these without warning, before
Jim could slow down. He jammed on his brakes instinctively to lessen the impact of the collision and at
the same time swerved. A sickening, slithering lurch
told of the inevitable skid on the wet chalk road. The
next moment there was a grinding, rending crash of
metal, as the radiator of the saloon buckled against
the lorry's front wheel. The lorry heeled, like a cap-
sizing boat, seemed to quiver a second uncertainly,
then settled over on its side, shooting gravel, kit,
tarpaulin, and the three eldest Marigolds in one heap
on the wet and muddy turf by the roadside.

Norah was the first up. Hatless, with her mackintosh split as far as the belt, she struggled to her feet,
and ran to extricate Biddie, who was wallowing under
several hundredweight of gravel, as helpless as a May
beetle on its back.

" Hurt?" she queried briefly.

" No, but Pat is, I think."

" Nothing—I banged my nose on the side. It'll stop
bleeding in a minute. Look out for the kids," from
behind a somewhat inadequate handkerchief, Patsy
spluttered reassuringly.

Without needing a second bidding, Norah ran to
the front of the lorry. A sudden fear had shot into her
mind. As she came level with the driver's cab, however,
she drew a breath of relief. The nasty, uneven sound
of the racing engine had ceased. Jim must have

switched it off, so preventing the horrible danger of fire. She was vaguely aware of a broad-shouldered, hatless, elderly man climbing out of the wrecked saloon, but her thoughts were entirely with Pixie and Mary.

The lorry looked queer on its side. There was something unnatural and unnerving about the great wheels in the air, and the fact that the door leading into the driver's seat was so far up, now, out of reach. Heedless of mud and oil and her own scared wonder of what she might find there, Norah was preparing to scramble up to it, when it opened towards the sky, and Pixie's copper head, very tousled, appeared over the edge, peering oddly. Norah saw she had a rapidly darkening black eye.

" Oh, Pixie, are you all right?" she asked breathlessly.

" Yes, I'm all right—I think." Pixie did not seem very certain. " Ooh, Norah, do help. I b'lieve Jim's dreadfully hurt or something. He won't answer us when we speak to him, and Mary's glasses are broken all over her face, so she can't look and see. Oh, do help us to get out—quick, because I'm sure something ought to be done about Jim."

CHAPTER XXII

No Marks for Inspection

" The ambulance is coming. I can see it at the bottom of the hill now. My chauffeur must have found a place from which to telephone quicker than we expected."

The tall, grey-haired, kindly-looking man, whose car had caused the accident, came over to the little group of Marigolds gathered about Jim Willox, and looked down at them anxiously.

" Thank goodness!" Biddie remarked simply, without looking up. She was busy bathing a nasty cut on the young Scoutmaster's forehead. Norah, who was kneeling with his head on her knees, bent forward and pulled the thick blanket closer round him.

" I wish he'd regain consciousness," she said in a worried tone.

" Better if he doesn't. He won't feel the jolting in the ambulance so much. I'm pretty certain he's got some ribs twisted as well as a broken leg. The steering wheel must have jammed him," Biddie explained.

" Shall I keep on rubbing his hands?" Pixie asked.

" No, you can leave that, now. Get Patsy to doctor

that eye of yours, if she's through with Mary. It's swelling no end, kiddie," Norah remarked anxiously.

" Oh, that's all right." Pixie, usually the first to make a fuss, seemed determined to be helpful. " It doesn't hurt much."

Before anyone could argue with her the white-painted ambulance from a local Cottage Hospital drew up, and a capable-looking nurse, with two tall men in uniform, came hurrying over the grass.

Norah laid Jim's head gently back on an improvised pillow of coats, and stood up to report.

" We had an awful job getting him out, and he did come to for a few minutes—only his leg hurt so he fainted again," she explained.

After a brief examination, while the ambulance men were lifting Jim gently on to their stretcher, the nurse confirmed Biddie's diagnosis.

" He's got a broken leg and concussion, but he'll get over it, you needn't worry. None of you are the lad's relations, I suppose?"

Then, as they agreed they were not, the nurse added:

" He'll have to go to hospital, of course, and may be there some time. If you can give me the address of his home, none of you need come down now, I think."

While Norah was writing out Jim's address, she added:

" That is, unless you've got any hurts yourselves that need attending to?"

She had just caught sight of Mary, whose face, decorated with at least seven strips of plaster, was certainly startling.

"No—she's all right, nurse—only scratches where her glasses broke," Patsy explained, grinning. "She had the sense to shut her eyes and keep them shut, so there's no real harm done."

When the ambulance had driven off, the owner of the blue car looked the Marigolds over with approval, and a twinkle of amusement he could not hide.

"Well, I will say you're a plucky lot of youngsters, and you know how to keep your heads in an emergency. Now tell me, where do you come from, and how do you intend getting back there?"

"We come from Oakleigh, but we want to get to Barham Towers, near Welworth," Norah explained. "You see, we're entering for a Patrol Competition."

Their new acquaintance looked rather doubtful.

"Can you possibly carry out that plan—now?" he asked.

"I don't know," Norah looked at her watch, and frowned. "My goodness, it's past twelve already! If only there were a bus, or something. But this is such a desperately lonely place, why, not a single car's passed us yet, since we crashed."

"I wasn't thinking so much of the difficulty of getting to Welworth—I was thinking that you've all had a nasty shaking and probably ought to go home to bed," the stranger insisted.

Dirty, war-worn and bedraggled, the Marigolds

grinned back at him. Somehow he was a person who inspired confidence.

"We *must* get to Welworth somehow. This competition's absolutely vital to us as a patrol," Norah told him.

Very briefly she explained the circumstances, doing her best, meanwhile, to rub stains of mud and blood off her tunic with a handful of rough grass.

. . . .

"Sixth Oakleigh Company—the Marigold Patrol? I suppose you know you're very late?" an overworked and rather cross lieutenant, with the scarlet orderly band on her arm, turned to look without enthusiasm at five almost incredibly untidy, dirty, red-headed Guides.

The leader, distinguished by her stripes alone, since she actually wore no hat, nodded casually.

"We'd a sort of idea we might be. Can you tell us where we belong to go now, at all?" she drawled in a soft, Irish brogue.

"Stand D. 15. It's down there, on the far side of the Rally Ground. For goodness' sake, run or you'll get yourself all mixed up with the judges. You'll find instructions on the fence."

"Right, thanks very much!" with a salute that was smarter than could have been expected, the leader turned away, and, each clutching some unrelated and dishevelled piece of equipment, the patrol took to its heels and ran—the smallest Guide and even smaller recruit, as the lieutenant noted with fresh disgust, holding hands like a couple of Brownies.

All round the field, patrols that had travelled from far and near, arriving early, and preparing themselves at leisure for the important moment of inspection by the County Commissioner, were already drawn up, each within the stand allotted, against the iron railing fence, where hung neat cards of instructions. D. 16 and D. 14 looked with curiosity and some amusement, as the Marigolds panted up the field. Norah, however, was in no mood to take notice of them or their opinions. She was fighting in a lost cause, with her back to the wall and every drop of the Irish blood in her veins answered to the stress of so grand an emergency.

How they had got there at all, by means of buses, trains and finally a lift on a baker's cart, was an Odyssey in itself. Their lunch had been eaten on the way, and they had managed to wash a portion of the dirt off themselves at a tap on a wayside station. But gravel and chalk and motor oil are all difficult things to cope with. Though they had done a noble best, their appearance would have made any leader except Norah throw up the game in despair. Norah, however, refused to be beaten.

" Dump the kit. That's right. Patsy, here's the clothes brush. Biddie, here's a comb. Mary, take your stockings *off*, those ladders are past mending, they've all sprung again, where I sewed them up in the train. Pixie, will you lend me your hat, just for inspection? It may not be noticed if you haven't one, but they'll spot me at once."

When, five minutes later, the whistle blew which called the waiting patrols to attention, the Marigolds stiffened with the rest. Norah, bending forward, whispered down the line:

" Remember, not a word, unless the County Commissioner asks you a question. If you speak without being spoken to, I'll scrag the lot of you. And, don't forget, a good turn you *tell* about doesn't count as a good turn at all."

Patsy, Biddie and Mary nodded. Pixie choked on a giggle. The sight of tall Norah in a hat at least three sizes too small, and belonging to herself, struck her as the funniest thing she had ever seen.

For some reason it did not appear to strike the white-haired, erect old lady, wearing County Commissioner's cockade and cords, who presently, with her impressive staff of Division and District Commissioners behind her, strode down the field from Stand D. 14, in the same light. Not the faintest flicker of amusement showed in her steel grey eyes, as she answered Norah's salute.

" Marigold Patrol, 6th Oakleigh Company?" she asked, in a deep voice that, somehow, reminded them all of Lady Royston.

" Yes, madam."

" You're a school company, aren't you?"

" Yes, madam."

" Hmph!" the County Commissioner's eyes swept

over the five deplorable figures of fun. They flickered for a second on Mary's much plastered face, and Pixie's bruised eye. She turned back to Norah and for a second that much harrassed leader hoped she meant to ask the question which alone made the giving of their most legitimate excuses etiquette. However, she merely snorted again:

"Hmph! Very poor turn out. You're thoroughly untidy, all of you. Where's your kit?"

"Here, madam." Norah stepped forward and displayed two muddy groundsheets, a dishevelled blanket, and a first-aid case denuded of most of its contents. ("Surely now she'll guess — she must," thought Norah.)

But the Commissioner merely snorted again:

"No marks for inspection," she said briefly.

"But, madam——" Pixie's wail broke out irrepressibly.

Norah quelled her with one glance. She subsided.

Strictly at the salute, the patrol waited while the Guiders of the staff passed them. Norah felt that some of these were curious and all more sympathetic than the County Commissioner had been.

"Of all the mean, unfair, mouldy old——" Patsy was beginning fiercely.

Norah cut her short.

"Don't waste time grousing, my infant. We didn't deserve a mark and we haven't got one. But it doesn't matter. We're going to *win* this competition all the same."

" But, Norah, how can we possibly?" Pat asked.

" By not losing one mark in any of the other classes, not one, d'you hear? There were five for inspection and we've got to make them up on the rest of the programme. Come on, Marigolds; the Jolly Roger's still nailed to the masthead. This afternoon it's *death but no surrender*!"

CHAPTER XXIII

The Desert Island

" Well, I think people are jolly decent, that's all. Fancy that patrol from Chagleigh lending us their signalling flags! I felt honestly ashamed to be able to read the message when they couldn't!" Norah remarked, strolling back to the Marigolds' Patrol base with Patsy and Biddie. " Hallo, you-all, how did you get on with your bit?"

" Ever so well!" Pixie beamed. " We had to pretend Mary was quite new to Guides, an' I had to explain to her all about the Tenderfoot Test, while a Commissioner listened."

" So I didn't have to look at anything," Mary rejoiced. " I was so afraid it'd be knots or something I couldn't see to do."

" An' the Commissioner person asked us if we'd been in a free fight, cos of our faces—she was ever so funny—we liked her. And I said, no, but we'd had a most thrilling accident coming here and done real first aid, just like in an adventure book, and she was ever so interested."

" Pixie!" Norah was appalled. " You never went

and showed off about it? I told you specially not to say a word."

"Only at inspection," Pixie pouted. "I didn't think it'd matter when a person asked us."

"Truly, we had to tell. It wouldn't have been polite not to," Mary said, closing the discussion, with one of her odd little touches of dignity.

Norah shrugged, and studied the list of competitions they had been given earlier in the afternoon.

"Inspection, we've done that—first aid, child nursing, signalling and recruit test—we've done all those. It's 'Surprise Test' now, and after that—oh, joy and bliss—we have tea; and while we're having tea, my children, we'll have to decide how in the world we get ourselves home from here. But don't let's worry now. If I'm not much mistaken we'll need all the brains we can muster for this next item."

Norah's premonition was justified. A whistle from the Judges' stand presently summoned patrol leaders racing across the field at the double. Anxiously their patrols, gathered in little knots, waited and watched the dark square of navy uniforms, blocked solid in front of the raised wooden platform, under the elm trees in the far corner of the field. After five minutes there was a stir, the groups broke up, and the leaders hurried back. The Marigolds were confounded to read on Norah's face a look of real consternation.

"Desert islands," she said briefly. "We're supposed to be wrecked on one of the outer Hebrides, with only the kit we've got with us now. We're to fix up our own particular stand with a shelter and fireplace, and all the gadgets we can, and then, when the Judges come round, two of the patrol are to do a five minutes' instructive dialogue."

" What on earth about?" Patsy asked.

" Anything on the face of the earth that we think may be 'interesting to other Guides'. 'Something that'll teach us anything we didn't know before in an interesting way,' the Commissioner said."

" Glory!"

They stared at each other.

The sunny field, the moving figures, the very line of the fence rail, seemed to swim before their eyes. All five were very, very tired, and now, for the first time, they realized it.

" We've *got* to be original," Norah said desperately. " It's our absolutely only chance."

" Could we talk about queer sayings—you know—how they came to be used—like 'letting the cat out of the bag ' or ' buying a pig in a poke '. Captain told us once, didn't she?" Patsy suggested tentatively.

" Yes, but I can't remember what she said; can you?" Norah clasped her head.

" If only Andrea was here she could tell about foreign places," Pixie wailed.

" Or about music," Mary added.

" Norah, I could tell a lot about herbs," Biddie volunteered.

Norah looked up, stared at her, then suddenly beamed.

" I've got it! Not herbs only—Gipsy lore—you
know; all the things Ellie's told us about. Oh, what
fun! I'll put the blanket round my head and shoulders,
and be an old gipsy woman and Patsy can be the
Guide, asking me things. Quick, let's make a list of
the bits of information to get in. Mary can write them
down while we get on with the desert island, or Mary,
if you can't see to write, let Pixie. You can help with
knocking in tent pegs. They're big enough for you
to find without your glasses!"

.   .   .   .

" Why, my dearie, I knew I'd be meeting friendly
folki this morning. And how did I? Well, I'll tell
you. As I came down the wood path by now, what
do I see but a water-wagtail, right in my way." Norah,
always a good actress, was not in the least perturbed
by the group of judges, who, having inspected the
patrol's very adequate little shelter of groundsheets,
trench fireplace, and other desert island paraphernalia,
were looking rather puzzled by her announcement
that she was " Mrs. Gerania Smith, an old, wise
gipsy woman."

Pat, rather pink and self-conscious, asked stiffly:

" What has a wagtail to do with your meeting
friends, Mrs. Smith?"

" Surely, pretty lady dear, the wagtail's the gipsy
bird. We say, when one crosses the path, ' *Ak'o
romano cheriklo: dikasa i Kalen*', which, in gorgio language, means, ' Lo, here is the Romany bird—we
shall meet gipsies.' And then we say, ' Is it any kin

to me, it will fly, it will fly '—but the bird I saw by now, it just hopped off my path, so I knew it wasn't any gipsy of my own tribe, but strangers that were wood folk and friendly."

"That's a very queer superstition. Why do you call the wagtail the gipsy bird, Mrs. Smith?" Pat waded on with her part.

"Oh, that's a very old ancient story, my dear." Biddie, Pixie and Mary could hardly suppress a smile, so exactly had Norah captured Ellie's sing-song whine. "They do say, among the Romanies that when Lady Mary was fleeing into Egypt with the blessed Holy Child, soldiers followed hard behind. The quail, that saw them pass, flew after her, and it called to the soldiers, ' *Aqui-vai*, *Aqui-vai* '—' here they go, here they go '. But the wagtail, that over-heard the wickedness, he hopped along and he swept the desert sand over her footprints with his long tail, so that the soldiers could find no track. They do say Lady Mary cursed the quail, the way he can only cry those two words now, for ever, and the way he can't rise high nor fly far, but the little wagtail she blessed and made him lucky. Oh, yes, dearie, it's lucky to see a wagtail on the path in early morning."

"You know a lot of old legends, Mrs. Smith. Is it true gipsies believe an adder brings luck, too?" Patsy asked.

"Not till he's dead, dearie. You cut a dead adder in two halves with a whip or a stick—put his head on the right side of the road and his tail on the left.

Then you make your family to walk between the two—father first, mother next, down to the youngest child—it won't be long then before all of you's got a pocket full of gold."

" One more question, Mrs. Smith—what are the ' Gipsy Seven Sleepers '?"

" A'ko. The Gipsy Seven Sleepers, they're the hedgehog, the snake, the dormouse, the squirrel, the snail, the bee and the frog—what else, my dearie?"

" Nothing else, Mrs. Smith—except I'd be grateful if you'd tell me the gipsy's blessing again."

Norah turned to the judges:

" God send you be both branch and flower:
The Lord send us all a happy hour,"

she repeated softly.

. . . .

" Did they like it? Do you think they were interested? Or did it sound silly and boring?" Norah asked anxiously.

" They were thrilled," Biddie reported loyally, " and it didn't sound a bit silly—not nearly as silly as the patrol next door. *They* did a bit about the death of Nelson. It was quite fun, but everybody knows about that, don't they? It wasn't new."

" And now——" Norah stretched her arms above her head and yawned cavernously: " now for tea——"

" Which I should think you must be ready for, by the look of you all!"

At sound of the deep voice all five Marigolds turned.

" Lady Royston! Oh, how lovely of you to come. Why didn't you tell us? Where have you come *from*?" Norah asked, at once taken aback and delighted.

Lady Royston snorted.

" Hmph! I didn't tell you I was coming, for the good reason that, until lunch time to-day, I didn't mean to come. But when I got a 'phone call from your friend, Mr. Hewlett, to say the lorry you'd started in was smashed to smithereens and the man in charge of you was in hospital, I changed my mind. I guessed I should find *some* of you here, so I got Bridges to drive direct to the ground. I'll admit I'm relieved to find a complete patrol."

" You're sweet!" Norah squeezed her arm hard.

" Let me look at you. Mercy on us, what spectacles! Well, well. How have you done in the competitions? Failed at everything, I suppose?"

" ' No marks for inspection '," Norah admitted, " but we didn't do *too* badly at the other things, we hope."

" Indeed? I'm glad to hear it. Sit down and have your tea now. Here come the orderlies with it. What happens after tea?"

" A camp fire—and then the results and then we go home," Norah told her.

" With me," Lady Royston rapped out, so emphatically that they jumped.

" If you'll take us——" Norah began politely. Then suddenly laughed. " We'd love to be taken home by you," she admitted frankly. " We just couldn't imagine

how we were going to start, even, on our own. You're
our own particular special Patrol guardian angel in
disguise!"

" In very adequate disguise!" Lady Royston snorted,
but her eyes were kind.

. . . .

" The County Shield for the most efficient all-
round patrol goes this year to the Kingfisher Patrol
of 1st Chagleigh Company." The County Commissioner's voice rang out in a silence so complete that
the twittering of swallows as they skimmed low over
the circle of attentive, blue-clad figures, gathered
round the big camp fire, sounded startlingly loud.
" They have gained ninety-six marks out of a possible
hundred on the tests this afternoon—a very excellent
percentage."

Wholehearted clapping, and some hearty cheers of
congratulation, greeted the tall patrol leader who made
her way forward to receive the shield.

" They lost on their signalling—nothing else,"
Norah murmured. She felt she had to say something,
as she caught sight of the tired, grubby faces of the
two youngest Marigolds, now blank with bitter disappointment.

" Second—and only second one mark, come the
Marigold Patrol, of 6th Oakleigh." The County
Commissioner paused, and her eyes sought out the
hatless, red head of a startled patrol leader. " Guides,
I want to tell you something about this patrol. The
Marigolds have come second to-day, because no

marks could possibly be awarded to them for inspection. They lost their five marks at one swoop on that item. But I hear that when they set out this morning they were tidy and well-equipped. They had the misfortune to meet with a bad motor accident on the way—and I hear they proved themselves very efficient in dealing with it. They then were plucky enough to come on here and to take their chance, telling nobody what had happened. If a gentleman who witnessed the accident had not telephoned a message for me to Barham Towers House early this afternoon, no one need ever have known *why* the Marigolds lost five marks to-day. I have very much pleasure in announcing that, under the circumstances, a second prize has been awarded. Will the Marigold leader please come for it, now?"

There could be no question about the popularity of the judges' decision. As Norah, blushing scarlet with surprise and embarrassment, went forward to receive the beautiful framed copy of Margaret Tarrant's picture, " The Adventurers ", the applause nearly deafened her. The Kingfishers of 1st Chagleigh were first to congratulate her as she returned to her place.

" I honestly don't feel we deserve the shield at all. You were marvellous," their leader told Norah, shaking hands heartily.

" Oh, rats! We owe you a lot for lending us those flags, ours were torn to shreds. I hope we meet again some day," Norah told her.

When at last they were packed comfortably into Lady Royston's car, and travelling homewards through the chequered evening sunshine of the quiet country lanes, the precious picture, with the County Commissioner's inscription on the back of the frame, firmly wedged between Norah and Patsy, Lady Royston looked them over quizzically.

"Well," she said, "I'd kept a bit of news for you people, in case you did very badly this afternoon. I had an idea you might need cheering up—but I see I was wrong."

"Do tell us. Is it another surprise?" Norah asked.

"A great surprise," Lady Royston admitted. "So great I could hardly believe it. I had a very long, detailed cable this morning, from Bucharest. Andrea's father is appointed to London. That means she'll be over here in a week's time and — what's even better—she and her mother and father will be coming to live, almost indefinitely, with me at Stone House."

CHAPTER XXIV

All's Well

" Steady—don't you be in a hurry now—easy does it. That's the style. All together, now, hold on behind, and down we go!"

Mr. Hewlett, warm, important, beaming and assisted by the entire Marigold Patrol, was overseeing a tricky job. This was neither more nor less than the conveying of a large, well-built and gaily painted caravan down the green slope under the cedar trees, that led to old Ellie's chosen pitch by the stream. Jim Willox, now out of hospital, though still limping a little, had borrowed a rough pony from a greengrocer friend, and now, with Mr. Hewlett leading the pony, while the Marigolds held on hard to the chains of the tilt and acted as a human brake, they were making good progress. Jim himself had been deputed to go ahead and see that all was in order on the proposed site.

It was the last afternoon of the summer holidays. Already the leaves were turning on the big beeches, and there was a nip in the air, morning and evening. The patrol, inventing an errand that should keep Ellie busy, had decided to fix her caravan where it was to remain for the winter. After weeks of hard

work it was ready for its occupant, down to the last
detail.

As it bumped to its resting place on a grassy mound
well above the level of possible flood-water from the
stream, sheltered by thick-growing trees on the north
and east, Norah sighed—a sigh of complete satisfaction.
Leaving Mr. Hewlett and Jim to unharness the horse,
she stood back and admired it, while the patrol clustered round her. They were in uniform, all of them,
for Miss Blagrove had called a company meeting at
her house that night, and Andrea and Mary were to
be enrolled. There was no doubt, now, that 6th Oakleigh would carry on. Miss Nesbitt, writing from
Devonshire, where she was spending her own holiday
in camp, had made that clear.

" Since, evidently, patrols can do good work on
their own, without interfering with school activities
or taking up an unfair share of the Guiders' time, I
shall be delighted for St. Bridget's Company to carry
on. I consider that there is absolutely no question
about it—the Guides have made good."

" Made good!"

Norah, looking first at the keen, smartly dressed
patrol, their green and yellow ties and marigold em-
blems gleaming in the sun, and then at the caravan,
gaily painted in the patrol colours of green, yellow and
warm, marigold orange, felt, with a sudden rush of
real humility, how lucky they had been. Right from
the first Saturday, when they had met Lady Royston,
circumstances had helped, not hindered them. There

had been kindly, eccentric little Mr. Hewlett, and then Andrea, coming home at the critical moment, and old Ellie, with all her odd, woodland wisdom.

" We've been lucky, oh, we *have* been lucky!" she thought.

" There! Sound as a nut, snug as a warren, and pretty as a picksher, ain't it, Jim? When that there old gipsy party comes home from market to-night, if she don't think fairies have been this way, she ought to. That's what I say!"

Mr. Hewlett mopped his brow, put his hands on his hips and considered the caravan with deep satisfaction.

" Tarred felt on the roof—a coat of creosote on the inside—and three good coats of paint outside. That's what I call honest work," he went on. " Nothing scamped, and nothing 'urried—con-sequently the weather ain't going to get in, and the good looks isn't going to wear off. You young ladies 'ave put in a very sound job and I'm proud of it."

" We could never have done it if you hadn't shown us how, and told us what materials to use," Norah told him.

" We've loved doing it. It's been such fun," Patsy added.

" Yes—and we've learned lots." Andrea looked at Mary and laughed.

Mary nodded.

" Lots *and* lots," she agreed.

" Let's look inside just once more before we leave it," Pixie begged.

One by one they climbed up the wooden steps and had a good look at the interior, which had called for so much care and thought in the past weeks.

The bunk bed was neatly made up with blankets and sheets they had gathered from their homes. There was a patchwork quilt, result of much patience and the free run of Lady Royston's ample rag-bag. On the shelf in the window, protected by a rail, were pots of geraniums, and the little cupboard held china in a gay pattern, and serviceable pots and pans from the 6d. store, not to mention a big canister of tea and another of sugar, and a jar of tobacco for Ellie's much loved, short clay pipe. From a hook on the wall, well secured, Mary's Mickey Mouse clock gave the last touch of homeliness by its loud and persistent ticking.

" There—we haven't forgotten a thing. Oh, I'm glad we kept it for a surprise! Ellie won't know until she gets back *what* sort of a house she's to have. Come on—let's go quickly, it'd spoil everything if we were here when she got back," Norah urged.

" Yes, and it's nearly four now. If we're going to tea with Mary, before we catch the Oakleigh bus, we haven't too much time," Patsy warned.

Mary gave a little skip.

At last, to-day, she was like other girls. She had a home again, and could ask friends to tea.

As they walked up through the woods, with many a lingering backward glance at the caravan, so bright, among the green shadows in the hollow, Norah looked at her kindly.

" Mary, child, what have you done with yourself? Do you know, you look positively *pretty* in uniform?"

Mary did, indeed, look very different from the skinny little object who had voted six months before to throw in her lot with the Marigold pirates. She had spent the holidays with Andrea and had grown and plumped out amazingly. Large horn-rimmed glasses, prescribed, at Biddie's urgent request, by a friend of Doctor Ormonde, a very clever occulist, had worked wonders, and so had Andrea's ruthless clipping and shampooing of her hair. Now, reduced to a short, well-brushed bob, it was seldom untidy, and smuts and ink stains rarely adorned a face healthily sunburnt.

At Norah's remark she stopped dead and stared up as if she had seen a ghost.

" I'm *not*," she said unbelievingly.

" Yes, you are."

Mary considered the matter deeply.

" Well!" she exploded at last. " I knew I could see to keep tidy now—but I never thought. Oh, it is funny!"

" What is?"

" Why, do you remember the Wishing Well? I *wished* I might stop looking odd—and—and—the water rose!"

" Yes, and Pixie wished she might save somebody's life, just once, and not tell about it after." Norah looked keenly at the once-spoilt child of the patrol. " Didn't you, Pixie?"

Pixie flushed and wriggled.

" Oh, Norah, that's not fair."

" Yes, it is. One doesn't boast to outside people, but a patrol can have its own secrets. I only heard from Jim Willox to-day that that morning when the lorry turned over *he* didn't switch the engine off, and poor old Mary couldn't, because she couldn't see. You did, didn't you, Pixie?"

" Well, yes. But it was easy, he'd shown us how. Only I couldn't find the switch at first. That's when I banged my eye on some sticky-out thing—a handle or something, I think."

" Anyway, you saved *two* lives, 'cos if that engine had gone on running it would have caught fire, and then we'd never have got Mary and Jim out—or you, for that matter. And you never told a soul, so *your* wish came true too," Norah said quietly.

At the top of the wood they waited to say good-bye to Mr. Hewlett and Jim, with many earnest thanks for their help, and walked on, down the long drive to the little, white-washed lodge by the gate, where Mary and her mother were to live.

Late snapdragons and asters made a riot of colour in the tiny garden. The bike Mary had inherited from Andrea stood, newly painted and polished, in the little porch. Hanging in the latticed window, open to the afternon sunshine, a big roomy cage swung to the breeze.

" Why, it's Aucassin and Nicolette—the love-birds we won at the fair!" Andrea exclaimed.

Mary nodded.

"Pixie's given them to me, 'cos now I've got a home," she said, and added, as she led the way in, "a real home again, and to *last*."

Norah and Andrea lingered in the porch a moment or two. In the green shadow of the honeysuckle that covered it, their eyes met and they smiled. Andrea slipped her hand under the folds of the new green and yellow tie—the tie that distinguished her already as the St. Bridget's schoolgirl she would to-morrow become.

"Here, take it, I'd like to be enrolled with this one, if I may," she said softly. "I've worn it all the time. To-morrow I'll be able to wear it where it'll show."

Norah took the shining trefoil and slipped it into her emblem-pocket.

"Glad?" she asked.

Andrea nodded.

"It's being a lovely day, isn't it? Sort of all the things we've wanted coming out right at once."

"Yes, I'm not sure if it's most like the end of a story, or the beginning of one. Are you?"

Andrea smiled.

"Maybe it's a bit of both," she said.